LOIS LENSKI

San Francisco Boy

Other Books by Lois Lenski

Autobiographical

A LITTLE GIRL OF NINETEEN HUNDRED

Historical

PHEBE FAIRCHILD, HER BOOK
A-GOING TO THE WESTWARD
BOUND GIRL OF COBBLE HILL
OCEAN-BORN MARY
INDIAN CAPTIVE
BLUEBERRY CORNERS
PURITAN ADVENTURE

Regional

BAYOU SUZETTE
STRAWBERRY GIRL
BLUE RIDGE BILLY
JUDY'S JOURNEY
BOOM TOWN BOY
COTTON IN MY SACK
TEXAS TOMBOY
PRAIRIE SCHOOL
MAMA HATTIE'S GIRL
CORN FARM BOY
SAN FRANCISCO BOY
FLOOD FRIDAY
HOUSEBOAT GIRL
COAL CAMP GIRL

SAN FRANCISCO BOY

by Lois Lenski

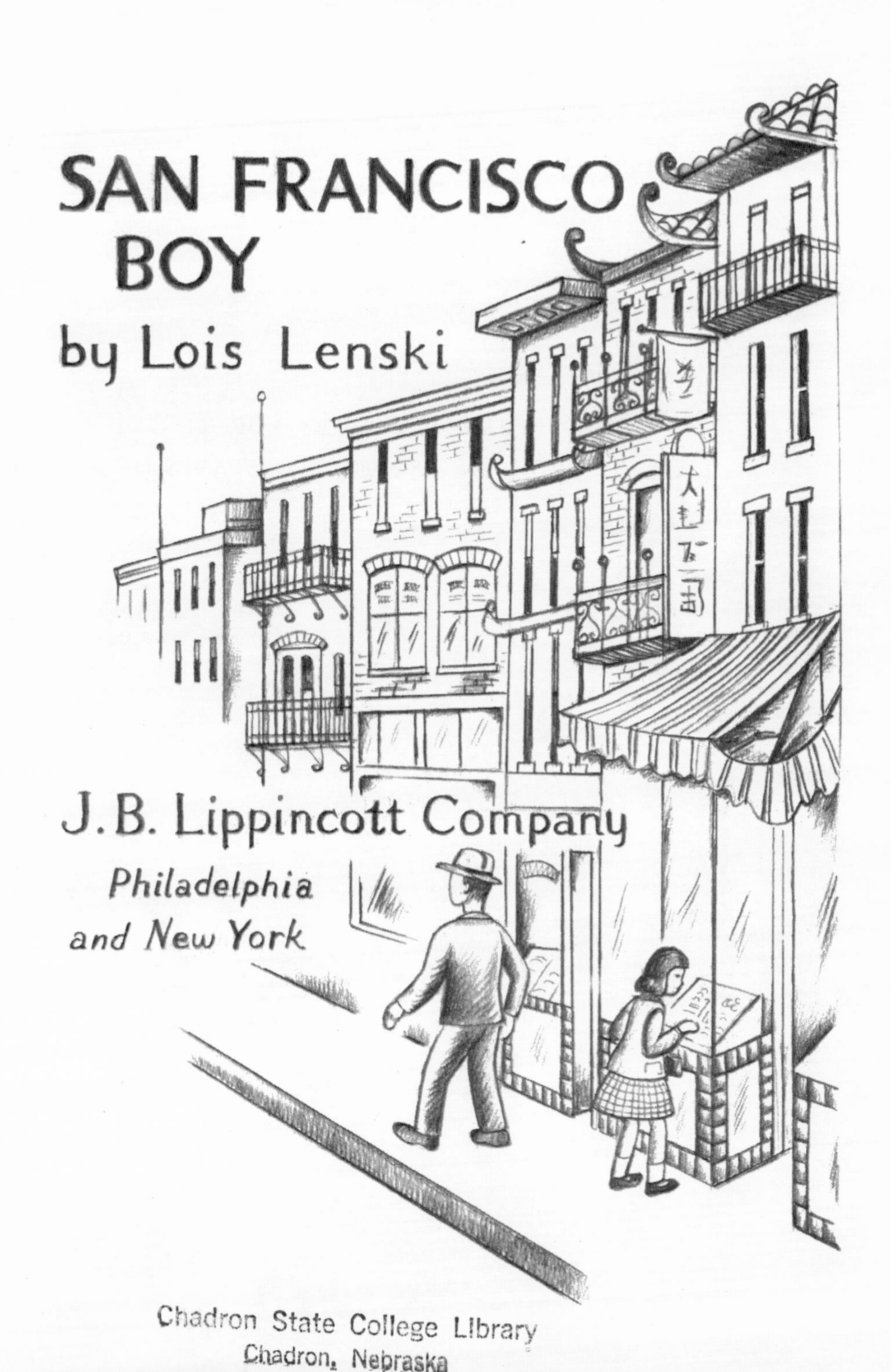

J. B. Lippincott Company

Philadelphia and New York

LITHOGRAPHED IN THE UNITED STATES OF AMERICA

Fifth Printing

Library of Congress Catalog card number 55-9506

For

my Chinese children,

with love

FOREWORD

Out on the west coast lies a beautiful city on many hills, San Francisco, surrounded by the waters of the Pacific. In the heart of the city, within a few crowded city blocks, an age-old civilization flourishes. Here East meets West in Chinatown.

Fourth-grade children in Commodore Stockton School, under the guidance of Mrs. Dina Gianni, their teacher, wrote me in December 1952, as follows:

"We have been reading the Roundabout America *books you have written, which tell how the children live, work and play in other parts of our country. We are Chinese children and live in Chinatown. We eat our rice and other foods with chopsticks and it is a lot of fun. We wear our Chinese costumes on certain days, for parades, for Chinese New Year, and for parties. Some of the children work after school. Some children work in the jeans factory, cutting threads off jeans and folding them. Others wash glasses and dishes in their parents' restaurants. Some children work in the laundry. They deliver, count and fold towels, put paper and cardboard on shirts and wrap bundles. Others count wrapping paper and stock baskets in the art stores. We go to Chinese school after American school and learn how to read, write and spell in Chinese.*

"Would you like to know more about us? Then come and visit us. Do you think other children would like to know how we live in Chinatown? We think it would be a good idea for you to write a book about us. We wish you good luck and good health."

What a wonderful invitation this was! Other letters followed during 1953–54, accompanied by beautiful drawings and paintings, depicting all phases of the children's daily lives. Not only were the Chinese children gifted in writing, but they were instinctive artists as well. I felt highly honored when they named their Book Club after me, and when it became an inspiration and stimulus to the reading of good books.

I visited San Francisco in June, 1954, and through the children came to know their parents and visit in their homes. I spent many happy days on the streets of Chinatown, observing, asking questions, filling notebook and sketchbook. I never lacked for a personal guide. Wherever I went, I could always hear a child calling, "Oh, Miss Lenski, can I show you Chinatown?" The children took me into the art shops, bakeries, grocery, fish and poultry stores, factories and homes. I always had an interpreter, and because the children were my friends, I drank many cups of tea and always met a warm welcome. I saw Chinatown from the point of view of the children who make their homes there. With their help, this book has been written.

It is no small task to study the background of an ancient culture as rich as the Chinese, and I make no claim of having done so. I have tried to understand the compromise between the old and the new, so intelligently worked out by the modern Chinese. I wonder why many of their customs and their basic philosophy of living, proven to be effective centuries ago, have not been adopted by the West. They long ago learned the art of living together and of easing the frictions of daily living. We still have much to learn from them.

The Chinese in San Francisco speak of themselves as "Chinese" and of the Caucasians who surround them as "Americans." I have followed this local custom. In my book, the word "Chinese" means "Chinese-American citizen."

Lois Lenski

Lutean Shores
Tarpon Springs, Florida
December 1, 1954

Map of a Portion of Northern California
Showing SAN FRANCISCO ~
Setting of the story.

CONTENTS

There was presented to me a
plum
And I gave back a precious
stone—
Not as a return for it
But that our friendship might be
lasting.

—Old Chinese friendship song

CHAPTER I

A Walk in the City

"Oh, look!" cried Mei Gwen. "There's the shop where Grandmother buys her fish."

Mei Gwen pulled her two younger brothers across the street. Frankie was seven and Freddie six. Every day after school, Mei Gwen met them in the schoolyard and took them to the jeans factory where their mother worked. Her elder brother, Felix, walked ahead. It was hard to keep up with him, for the streets of Chinatown were very crowded. The children stopped in front of the Yet Sang Fish Shop. Mei Gwen held her nose. She did not like the smell of fish.

Mei Gwen, who was nine, wore her black hair in two braids, with bangs in front. Her sweater was bright red and her wool skirt was pleated. Her face was serious as she kept her eyes on her younger brothers.

They looked in the show window. Strange-looking fish, large and small, were lying on platters and hanging from hooks. Below the show window, inside the tile-covered walls, were two glass-fronted tanks, low on the sidewalk. In one were live frogs, in the other, live turtles. Frankie and Freddie crouched down to look. They pointed their fingers at the turtles. Felix knelt in front.

"Do you remember the turtle I had in Alameda?" he asked.

"No, Elder Brother," said Mei Gwen. "That was so long ago."

"I will tell you how I found it," said Felix. "One day I was walking in my garden near the tomato plants. I kicked up some dirt and what do you think I saw?"

The little boys' eyes opened wide with wonder.

"I saw a turtle sleeping. I picked it up," Felix went on. "I touched its back—its shell was very hot. It was hot, I guess, from sleeping in the sun. It looked like an old turtle."

"Was it as big as these?" asked Freddie, pointing.

"Yes, it was a big one," said Felix. "It was about eight inches long."

"Where did it come from?" asked Frankie.

"I don't know," said Felix. "It must have crawled into my garden during the night from some other place. Maybe it came through a crack in the fence."

"Did I see it?" asked Frankie.

"Yes, I showed it to you," said Felix. "I put the poor turtle in water to cool it off. I put it in the pool with the fish." He looked up at his sister. "Remember I told you we had a fishpool in our yard?"

"Yes," said Mei Gwen, "I remember. You talk about it all the

YET SANG FIS

time. What happened to your turtle? Did you eat it?"

"No," said Felix sadly. "About six months later my turtle died. I buried it under the cherry tree because I found it near the tree. The tomato plants were near the tree, too. I was so sorry and very sad. I had so much fun with my turtle and he was such a good pet."

"People don't make pets of turtles in the city," said Mei Gwen. "They buy them and eat them. They make soup out of them."

"But I don't want you to forget Alameda and the fishpond," said Felix.

The little boys pointed their fingers at the frogs in the next tank. They clapped their hands to make the frogs jump. One large frog sat very still and did not move.

"Look at him," said Mei Gwen. "How mean and angry he is. He's staring at me."

Suddenly the frog puffed out its cheeks, made a loud noise and jumped. The boys laughed.

"He wants to get after me," cried Mei Gwen. "Make him stop." The frog sat still again and did not move. "He's staring at me, I tell you."

"He won't hurt you," said Felix. "He can't get out."

Mr. Ben Lum, the fish man, came to the door and smiled.

"Tell that frog to stop staring at me, Mr. Lum," said Mei Gwen.

"It's your red sweater," said the fish man. "Frogs don't like red. Better go home and change it."

Mei Gwen smiled. Was Mr. Lum teasing her? "If I wear my old yellow one, will he stare at me then?"

"No," said Ben Lum, grinning. He went indoors, put a glove on his hand, reached into the tank and picked up the frog.

"Come, let's go!" cried Mei Gwen hastily. "He's taking the frog *out!* He's going to put it on top of me!"

"Don't be so scared," said Felix. "The poor frog won't hurt you. He's just putting it somewhere else."

"Come, let's go." Mei Gwen took the little boys by the hand and hurried along the street.

"Frogs won't hurt you," said Felix, catching up. "Once I had some tadpoles . . ."

"Oh, stop talking about your old fishpond," said Mei Gwen. "I'm tired of hearing about it. You and all your pets out there in Alameda! We're in San Francisco now, and everything is different."

"I like it better in the country," said Felix. He walked slowly, his hands buried deep in his pants pockets.

"Alameda is not country," said Mei Gwen. "It's a town—the houses are close together there. Mother told me so."

"To me it was like country," said Felix sadly. "They always have grass in the country. . . ."

"Grass? Who wants grass?" asked Mei Gwen.

A man from the Lotus Garden Restaurant passed by, balancing a trayful of food on top of his head. He entered the door of an office and went up the stairs. He was taking a hot meal to some of the workers.

The children came to the Sang Sang Poultry Shop and stopped. Live pigeons strutted back and forth in one show window, and dressed chickens hung from hooks in another. At the curb, a man was lifting crates of live chickens down from a truck. On the side of the truck a sign read: SANG SANG POULTRY RANCH, Walnut Creek, California. The man carried the crates into the open door and piled them on top of each other against the wall. Loud clucking and cackling could be heard, as feathers flew.

"Let's look at the pigeons," cried Freddie.

"I want to see the chickens," said Frankie.

"No," said Mei Gwen firmly. "We must turn back now." She pulled her little brothers along. "We cannot stop and look in every window. Mother will be waiting for us. She will say we are late again."

The children made their way slowly through the crowded street. Grant Avenue was a fascinating place. Gift shops, butcher shops, stationery and bookstores, groceries and herb stores stood

side by side, with open wall-shops and flower stands at the street corners. Pagoda-like cornices in bright reds and greens towered above the jutting balconies on upper floors.

Mei Gwen knew all the shops, although she had lived in the city for so short a time. All summer long she had gone shopping with Grandmother Yee and had carried things home in Grandmother's shopping bag. Grandmother said that a girl of nine was old enough to learn housekeeping, and the first part of housekeeping was buying supplies.

Mei Gwen loved to look in the windows as much as any one. She knew the Wah On Herb Shop where Dr. Low sold Grandmother the medicine when Frankie had a bad cold. She knew the Art Goods Shop where Aunty Rose bought her imported Chinese costume and embroidered slippers. She knew the bookshop where Father bought Chinese writing books, brushes and ink box for Felix when he started to Chinese school. She knew the Importers Shop where Aunty Kate's friends bought Chinese vases for Christmas and wedding presents. And she knew which grocery store had the best Chinese vegetables. But she could not take time to show the little boys all these things.

"I'm hungry," said Freddie.

"I'm hungry too," said Frankie.

"We will make only one more stop today," said Mei Gwen. She led the boys around the corner into a narrow alley. "Do you smell something good?"

"Um! Um!" sniffed Frankie.

The Wo Lee Noodle Shop faced on the narrow alley. As the children walked in the open door, Mr. Roy Jung came to greet

them. He was a good friend of Father's and knew the children well. He wore a white cap and apron, and his face, arms and clothes were dusty with white flour. He greeted the children and filled their hands with Fortune cookies. Each rolled-up cookie, when broken open, held a tiny paper with a "fortune" printed on it. The children opened theirs and Felix read them:

"It is better to keep a friend than to have a dollar."

"Good sense is the master of human life."

"Better not to speak at all than to say what is useless."

"Good! Good!" chuckled Mr. Jung, as he went back to his work. He and a helper were dusting a long, wide strip of dough with cornstarch, then folding it up in a neat pile, ready to be cut by hand with a large knife into noodles. The children thanked Mr. Jung and walked out.

"Let's go see Father," said Freddie.

"Just for a minute," said Mei Gwen.

A rear door to the Lotus Garden Restaurant, where Father worked, stood open in the alley just beyond. The little boys ran over and entered.

"Fish!" sniffed Mei Gwen, holding her nose. "They're always cooking fish. Oh, how I hate the smell of it."

The restaurant kitchen was a busy place, neat and spotlessly clean. Many tables held plates on each of which lay an uncooked fish. Baskets and bowls in orderly rows contained chopped-up vegetables, meats, seasonings and sauces, ready for special orders. Waiters in white coats passed back and forth, their arms loaded with filled porcelain and pewter bowls and dishes. At the huge stove in a far corner, the children saw Father busy at work. He was head cook and could not be interrupted. When one of the waiters spoke to him, he turned, smiled at the children, and lifting his hand, pointed to a clock on the wall.

"He wants you to go to the jeans factory, Younger Sister," said Felix. "And it's time for me to go to Chinese school."

The children came out of the narrow alley into the street again. Hand in hand they stood at the corner waiting for the traffic light to change.

Suddenly a girl a little younger than Mei Gwen passed by. She, too, had younger children in tow, a brother and sister. In Chinatown, the older children are always responsible for the younger ones. The girl stared at Mei Gwen, then lifted her chin and walked on ahead.

"Who is she?" asked Felix.

"Oh, that's the girl we pass on the stairs at home every day," said Mei Gwen. "They live on the second floor in our apartment house. Her father works at the Sun Sun Laundry on Mason Street. I've seen her lots of times, but she never speaks to me."

"People in the city are not friendly," said Felix. "Even those in our own apartment house never speak to us. Nobody tries to be kind to us. That's why I like Alameda better."

At the next corner, the children turned south, walked along by Portsmouth Square, turned again and came into Commercial Street. Felix waited at the corner until he saw Mei Gwen and the little boys go in at the door of Aunty Rose's jeans factory. Then he turned back, retracing his steps.

He had three long blocks to go, up Clay Street which was very steep, back to Stockton Street, where the Chinese school was located. Clay Street was not as steep as Sacramento, where the public playground was. Felix was learning the names of the streets at last. But he still hated the city, the crowds and all the noise. He still had no friends. The boys in public school and the boys in Chinese school did not like him. Even though he now knew the names of many of the streets, he was still afraid he might get lost. But, of course, he never told any one that.

The whole city was crowded and Chinatown most of all. There were too many people. Felix was always pushing into them, or being pushed off the sidewalk. At home, the Fongs' tiny apartment was overcrowded. Only three rooms for seven people. Felix did not like it. Chinese school was crowded too, and noisy. There was no peace and quiet at all. There were no trees to climb.

As he came into the schoolyard, Felix saw that all the boys

were there. They were bouncing balls against the bare walls of the high buildings around the yard. They were running, jumping, batting and yelling. When a noisy gong sounded, they all crowded to the door. Some went to upper rooms and some to lower. Felix stood in line with boys of his age. They went into a dark basement room, filled with large desks. Boys sat in two rows at one side, girls opposite. After all the pupils took their places, Mr. Ling, the teacher, passed out writing books. The room became quiet as they settled down to work.

Each pupil had a camel's hair brush for writing, and a brass ink box into which Chinese ink had been poured over silk floss, making a spongy moist cake. A printed copy sheet with Chinese characters on it was inserted between double rice-paper sheets in the writing books.

Felix held his brush in a vertical position between thumb and first finger. The other fingers grasped the handle, while the ball of his hand rested on the table. He breathed deeply, working hard to trace the strokes carefully. Each symbol was different, and there were thousands of them to be memorized. There was no alphabet making words as in public school, where he had learned to read English.

Felix Fong grew very discouraged. Would he ever learn to write? It was hard to have to read and write two languages. But Father said a Chinese boy could not do business in or out of Chinatown unless he knew both languages.

Suddenly out of the corner of his eye, Felix saw something moving. The boy in the next seat was passing something over to him. Felix reached out and took it. It was a comic book. Dared he look at it, while the teacher's back was turned? Mr. Ling was writing Chinese characters on the blackboard and explaining the order in which the strokes should be made. From across the hall, Felix could hear a din of voices. Children in another grade were reciting a lesson aloud in unison. This was the way they learned to read.

Pretending to be busy writing, Felix glanced now and then at the book on his lap. Reading a comic was easy—and funny too! The people did such crazy things. They leaped on horses and crossed high mountains. They jumped off steep places without getting hurt, they even rode rockets to the moon! They were always defending themselves against wicked enemies.

Suddenly, Felix came back to earth with a thud. He felt a ruler slap sharply across his shoulders. The comic book was whisked

away and thrown into the waste basket. A volley of Chinese words woke Felix from his dream. All the pupils were looking at him and tittering.

"Seventy-eight is your highest mark in writing, Felix Fong, sixty your lowest," Mr. Ling was saying. "Now you must do ten more pages of tracing for punishment."

Felix groaned. He could say nothing in his defense. He wished he had not taken the book from Sammy Hong, but it was too late now. There was nothing to do but stay after school and finish the ten extra pages.

When he came out of school at last, it was eight o'clock. He heard the clock in St. Mary's church steeple striking. Chinese school lasted from five to seven-thirty. School, school, all a boy's time must be spent in school. Public school from eight-thirty to three-thirty, then Chinese school on top of it. Would he ever be a scholar like his father?

Eight o'clock, nearly dark, and a cold wind blowing. Fog coming in from the bay. The city seemed always cold and rainy. The other boys had all gone home. But even if they were still there, or in the public playground on Sacramento Street, they were all strangers to him. Felix felt lonely and miserable.

He walked slowly along the street, uphill again. San Francisco was all hills. Home again—Mother and Mei Gwen and the little ones would have come back from the factory long ago. Supper would be over. Would they save something for him? Some left-over food for him to eat? Home again—would he ever feel at home in the damp, strange, noisy city?

He ran all the way up the three flights of stairs. He opened the apartment door with his key and went in. Father and Grandmother Yee were talking in the front room. Grandmother Yee, who lived with Aunty Kate, had come for the evening. She was short and plump, and always wore a black Chinese costume. She sat on the davenport knitting, never idle for a minute.

"My son," said Father, frowning. "Why are you so late?"

Felix hunted for words to explain.

"I have told you many times," said Father, "that if my sons look at, buy, or bring into my house a comic book, they will be severely punished. Since Mr. Ling has already punished you, I shall not do so. But you must understand that a comic book is an insult to one's artistic taste, a destroyer of moral sense and a lesson in evil ways. Such things you are to shun throughout life. If you do your work in school hours, you will not have to stay in. I will give you one more chance."

The smell of good food came to Felix from the kitchen. He greeted Grandmother and went out. There at the table sat the

baby, little Susie, two years old. She held her rice bowl in one hand and her tiny chopsticks in the other. She stopped eating long enough to look up and smile at Elder Brother. He bent over and kissed her cheek.

There was plenty of food left on the table. Mother spoke to the boy and poured out a cup of tea. Felix could hear the little boys in the middle room wrestling and boxing on the bunk beds. Before he sat down to eat, he washed his face and hands at the kitchen sink. Looking up, he glanced out the back kitchen window. Over the rooftops of thousands of white-walled buildings, night lights were shining like stars in the sky. Felix had never seen the bay so deep a blue before. Across it he could see the arching Bay bridge outlined in lights. Suddenly, for one short moment, his homesickness vanished. San Francisco was beautiful! He had never thought of it before.

Would he ever learn to love it?

CHAPTER II

A Friend and a Job

"Come on, let me in your game!" begged Felix.

"Naw, we don't want you. Go on away!" shouted Roger Loy.

Felix watched the boys playing baseball. He knew all their names now, but they never included him. He sat on the curb outside the public playground. Whenever the ball went over the high wire fence, he dodged through traffic, got it and threw it back. Sammy Hong, the boy who sat across the aisle in Chinese school, kept batting the ball over the fence.

Another high one went over.

"Go get it, Felix!" called Sammy.

But Felix was tired of being outfielder.

"Go get it yourself!" he answered. He walked into the playground and took up the bat, just as if his turn was next.

But the boys threw rocks at him and chased him out. Felix had a bunch of firecrackers in his pocket. He lighted them and threw them into the yard. They popped all over the place. The boys said, "Let's chase him." Felix ran away and they let him go. When they started their game, Felix crept back again.

While they were busy yelling, he took a long thin rope out of his pocket and tied it across the open gate. Then he hid behind the gatepost. Roger Loy came running out to get the ball. He did not see the string, so he tripped over it and fell. Felix ran away laughing. He looked back and made funny faces at Roger. The boys were tired of chasing him now. The ball game broke up and they stood talking together. Now and then they looked in his direction. He knew they were hatching up some mischief. He decided he had better clear out.

There was nothing to do but go home. Felix was hungry. He had to get something to eat before he went to Chinese school. He would be starved if he waited until after seven-thirty. Father would feed him at the restaurant if he went there, but he did not want to see Father. He could not tell Father that the boys would not let him play baseball. Father had said to him, "Get out there and play." When he told Father how mean the boys were, Father answered, "A Chinese boy has to learn how to protect himself." No—he did not want to talk to Father just now.

He'd rather go home, even though Mother was not there and the house was empty. Mei Gwen had taken Frankie and Freddie to the jeans factory after school as usual. There she had to be baby sitter to them and baby Susie and seven or eight others, the children of the women workers. Felix was glad he was not a girl. He'd hate to be a baby sitter all his life.

He unlocked the door and went into the apartment. The odor of damp clothes came to him. His mother had risen early that morning and done the washing before she left for work. Some of it was drying in the kitchen. The clotheslines on the roof did not hold it all. The front room was part parlor and part bedroom. It had a cot for Mei Gwen, a crib for Susie and a davenport that opened into a double bed for Mother and Father. The middle room was where the boys slept. It had a cot and a double bunk bed. The boys took turns sleeping on top. The kitchen was small and crowded. It had a gas stove, cupboards on the wall and a round table for eating. The icebox was on the tiny back porch.

The apartment was quiet and cheerless. Felix found some fish and rice in a steamer on the stove. He gulped the food down. It was only four o'clock—too early to go to Chinese school. Home was a terrible place with nobody in it. He walked through the hall and went out the front door, snapping the lock behind him.

He went slowly down the stairs. Passing the doors of the other apartments, he could hear voices. The man and woman in No. 4 were quarreling again. The little girl in No. 3 was crying. The door of No. 1 opened and old Mr. Wong came out. He had a skinny beard and wore a black skullcap. He leaned on his cane and talked to himself as usual. He did not see Felix at all.

The boy sat awhile on the front doorstep, watching the people and cars that passed. He felt friendless and alone. He remembered the good friends he had left behind in Alameda. There was Johnny Lew, and Jack Bailey the American boy, the three Wing boys, and Timmy who often came to visit his grandparents next door. There was always someone to play with, there was always something to do.

Felix looked down the street. Soon he saw Roger Loy coming. Roger had a stack of papers under his arm. Roger had a job—he was a paper boy. He had to deliver the *Call-Bulletin* to customers in stores and apartments.

Why couldn't he make a friend of Roger, Felix wondered. How could he make him a friend? He had just tripped Roger up on a rope. That was not a very good start. What could he do now to make Roger forget it?

All at once he remembered the motto on the paper in the Fortune cookie—*It is better to keep a friend than to have a dollar.* But how do you make a friend in the first place? *What is yours belongs to your friends. To make a friend, give him a gift.*

Where had he heard these sayings? From Father? Mother? Grandmother? He had been told them so often, they were a part of him now. Maybe they were a part of that "Chinese heritage" his parents were always talking about. Did those old sayings mean anything? Could he put them to use? If Roger Loy hated him, could he make him his friend? Could he share things with him, give him something of his very own, not something that would cost a lot of money—because his mother would have to earn it—but just some little thing?

Roger Loy was coming closer. He went into some of the doors, left a paper and came out. He came to the door of Felix' apartment house, glanced at Felix sitting on the doorstep, then up the steps he bounded. He had to take a paper to No. 5 on the third floor. He would be down again in a minute. It was now or never.

What can I give him? Felix thought quickly, as he felt in his pockets. All he had was a pack of firecrackers, which Uncle Fred had given him, and he had intended keeping until Chinese New Year. He wanted them himself, but he knew well that a gift is not a gift if it is something you want to get rid of. When Roger came down the stairs, Felix held the firecrackers out and smiled at him. It was a gift any Chinese boy would like. Roger looked at him in surprise.

"You didn't shoot them all off, then?" he said.

"No," said Felix. "I saved these for you."

Roger put them in his pocket and grinned in a friendly way. He wasn't mad at all. The tripping up at the playground was forgotten.

"How's the paper business?" asked Felix.

"Hard work," said Roger. "I have four blocks to take care of and thirty-two papers to deliver. They are so heavy to carry, I work fast to get rid of some of the load."

"Could I help you?" asked Felix.

Roger looked at him in surprise. He thought for a minute. "You mean you want a job?"

"Yes," said Felix.

"I need somebody to take my route when I get sick," said Roger, "and I'd like company when I'm well. I was wondering whom I could ask."

"I have nothing to do every day after American school is out," said Felix, "until Chinese school at five. Sometimes my father makes me come to his restaurant and wash dishes, but I'd rather help you."

"I'll speak to my route manager," said Roger, "and let you know tomorrow."

Felix had good news for the family the next night. He had a new friend and a new job. Father was very pleased. Mother, who never had much to say, smiled her approval. When the last grain of rice had vanished from the rice bowls and the chopsticks were laid aside, Father lectured the children on good manners at home and in public. This was the true preparation for job responsibility, he said. The children listened in silence, as the words sank in deeply.

The days passed more quickly now. No longer did Felix loaf around the public playground or beg the other boys to let him enter their games. As soon as public school was out, he met Roger Loy at the corner of Grant Avenue, where they received their papers from the newspaper truck. Felix went with Roger every day at first to learn the route. It was hard, as Roger had said, because there were so many stairs to climb, especially on Stockton Street. The boys had to leave the papers right beside the doors of offices, factories and apartments.

As soon as Felix learned the route, Roger let him take it alone one day. It was different without Roger. Felix had not realized what a cheerful, lighthearted boy Roger was. When together, the boys were always laughing and joking. Without Roger, there was no fun at all.

Felix started into an alley where he had two customers. The sun had begun to set and it threw dark shadows across the alley. Felix saw a queer-looking woman digging into a garbage can beside a dark doorway. Cats crowded about her. From a wire shopping cart, she took paper plates on which she placed fish and other food. Meowing cats came up to eat off the plates. The Cat Lady looked at Felix and smiled.

"The cats are happy if they have plenty to eat," she said.

Felix felt sorry for the cats, but the bright glint in the old lady's eyes made him uneasy. He shivered and felt spooky, so he hurried on. He dropped one paper in front of a doorway, then went to the next.

Joe Hong's door was three steps down. The place looked closed and there was no light. Felix knocked, for Roger had told him to collect. No answer came, so he started to leave the alley. The Cat Lady was gone now, but the cats were still eating the food she had given them. Uncertain what to do, Felix ran back to Joe

Hong's again. Still no light, still no answer. Should he leave a paper or not? What would Roger say if he did not collect? Joe Hong owed for two weeks already. While he was waiting, the door suddenly popped open. There stood Joe Hong, a sharp, thin little man with a frown.

"Why are you so late, boy?" he demanded. "Why can you not come on time?"

Felix blinked in surprise. He dared not say he had knocked twice before. He knew he must be polite. If a boy has good manners, he does not keep his elders waiting. He always treats his elders with respect.

"I am sorry, Mr. Hong," said Felix. "I will bring it earlier tomorrow."

The man went in and closed the door behind him.

Felix was glad to get out to the street again. Neon lights were blinking off and on. Cars were honking and people shouting. For once he liked the glare and noise. It was better than the dark alley. Policeman Mike walked by, swinging his club and whistling an Irish tune.

Felix stopped at the outdoor wall-shop at the corner. The shop was made up of shelves built against the outside wall of a building, closed at night with wooden shutters. In a little box-like booth, Mr. Chew sat on a stool reading a Chinese newspaper. He read the *Call-Bulletin,* too, and reached for the paper Felix handed out.

"You new boy," said Mr. Chew. "You feel good today?"

Felix nodded and smiled. Mr. Chew sold candies, fruits, souvenirs of all kinds, books and notions. He leaned over and gave Felix a handful of lichee nuts. Felix grinned and said, "Thank you."

He went into the next office building and hurried up the stairs. Would his legs ever get used to all the steps? No wonder Roger complained. The hallway was dark with only a dim light burning at the end. Felix could hardly see where he was going. He wanted to get out quickly. He hurried so fast that he tripped over a door mat and fell. He came down hard on his wrist.

The office door opened and an American businessman nearly stepped on him. "What's this?" he said. "Did you fall? Are you hurt?"

"Not much, thank you," said Felix. The man helped him to his feet. "I guess I'm O. K."

He rested a bit and went on to three more buildings. In each he had to go up long flights of stairs. It took him so long he was late for Chinese school and had to stay in again. That night he did not get his big dinner until nearly nine o'clock and he had to eat all alone.

Roger was very particular about the weather. He did not like rainy days at all, and always wanted Felix for company. The boys both wore raincoats and rain hats. They took shopping bags to put their papers in. They had to be careful to keep the papers dry, for nobody wanted to get a wet paper.

One dark, rainy day, Roger did not show up. Felix knew he must be sick, because he never failed to come whenever it was raining.

Felix started out bravely. He went into several office buildings. He tried to tell himself it was better to be inside where it was dry than outside where it was wet. But it was dark in the halls and the sound of the rain beating against the windows frightened him. Although he hated to admit it, he was scared in the dark and had told Roger so. He watched the rain pounding on the window and could not make up his mind to go outside. If only Roger had come to keep him company!

As he stood there, he thought of Alameda. He remembered a storm there long ago, when Freddie was little. The Fong family were all sleeping soundly in one big room. Suddenly, in the middle of the night, there was a rushing noise—thunder, rain and lightning all at once. Felix' bed was near the window and he woke up scared. He jumped, as lightning flashed across the room. He saw his mother get up, tuck the covers in around the younger boys, then go back to her bed. She did not know that Felix was awake.

Felix could not sleep. He saw shadows on the wall and they looked like terrible faces to the boy. He heard the clock go *tick tock, tick tock,* and he was very frightened. How happy he was when daylight came. The shadows disappeared, the storm was over, and everybody woke up. Felix wasn't scared any more and felt better. When he told his mother about his fright, she said a storm was nothing to worry about.

Now, walking in the dark office building, the boy heard the rain beating against the windows so hard he could not see out. The sound brought back all his old fears. He walked slowly on. Suddenly he thought people were following him. He turned and looked—they were hiding round a corner. He walked faster, then started to run. They were after him again. He dropped his

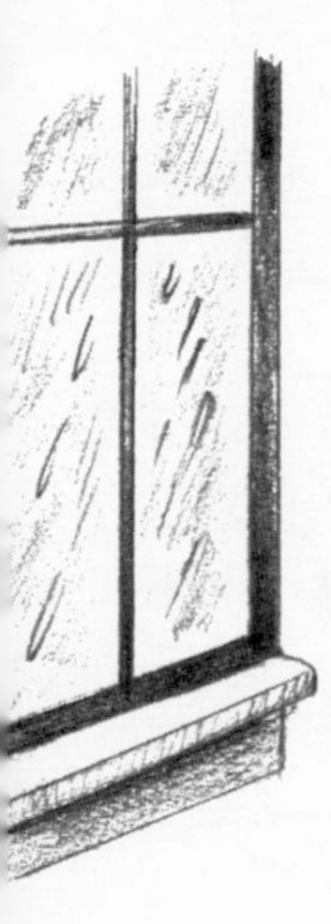

papers and rushed down the stairs. When he got to the bottom, he heard a loud laugh. Taking courage, he looked up the stairs behind him. There on a landing stood Roger, doubled up with laughter.

"Oh, Felix!" he cried. "It's only me! I was just trying to fool you." He came running down with Felix' bag of papers. "What did you drop your papers for?"

Felix' face was white and he could hardly speak. At last he said, "Please don't scare me any more, Roger."

"I did it on purpose," said Roger, "because I know you are scared in the dark. I want you to stop being so silly."

"I thought you must be sick," said Felix, "when you didn't show up today. We always go together on rainy days. But you weren't sick at all."

"I wanted to cure you of getting scared," said Roger again. "Did you collect from Joe Hong?"

"No," said Felix. "I went there twice. I knocked on the door both times and nobody came. Then the third time, Mr. Hong opened the door. He was there all the time."

"Did you ask him for the money he owes us?" asked Roger.

"No, I forgot," said Felix. "Mr. Hong was mad. He said I was late. He must have been taking a nap."

"The hardest part of this job is collecting the money," said Roger. "You must learn to be patient, always polite and patient."

"I don't like collecting money," said Felix. "I'm no good at it."

After that, Roger did the collecting with better results. Once a month he gave all the money to his route manager, who divided it. Each boy earned nine dollars a month. It was a proud day for Felix when he took his first money to Mother.

"I will start a bank account for you," said Mother. "Sometimes I will use some to buy your shoes, but most of this money is to be used for learning."

"More school?" asked Felix.

"Yes, my son," said Mother, "so you can be a scholar like your Father."

CHAPTER III

A Day in the Country

It was Saturday. Father had a day off and decided to go to the country with his friend, Ed Leong, from the Sang Sang Poultry Shop on Grant Avenue. They were to have a ride in Uncle Ed's truck and go to the Sang Sang Poultry Ranch at Walnut Creek. Felix and Mei Gwen called Mr. Leong "Uncle" because he was a close friend of the family. Father told the children they could go along on the trip. Mother would be at home all day to take care of the younger ones.

"In the city, we have no contact with the good earth and plants and animals," said Father. "We must not cut the cord that binds us to all living things. We will renew our acquaintance with Nature. We will spend a day on a ranch in the country."

"What is a ranch?" asked Mei Gwen.

"Don't you know?" asked Felix. "A ranch is where many

chickens are, and sometimes dogs and pigs and horses." He turned to Father. "Can we go to Alameda too? Can we stop and visit Cousin Hom?"

"The ranch is at Walnut Creek," said Father. "It is a long way from the city and we must let Uncle Ed decide the route. We are his guests. It is his truck and he will be driving."

Mother put her arm around Felix' shoulder. "Do not set your heart on stopping at Alameda, my son," she said. "Have all the fun you can at Walnut Creek."

Father and the two children walked to Grant Avenue to the poultry shop. Father carried his tea basket and Felix brought a large paper sack full of fish sandwiches. The poultry truck stood waiting at the curb, and near it stood Uncle Ed Leong. He was a fat, jolly man and he helped the children climb up in the cab. Felix sat in the middle and Mei Gwen sat between Father's knees. Soon they were on their way. The truck moved slowly through the crowded streets to the bridge entrance, then faster on Bay bridge itself.

"Do you remember when we went back to visit Cousin Hom in our Alameda house, Younger Sister?" asked Felix.

"I think so," said Mei Gwen. "It was hot and I took off my shoes and stockings, and got sticky things in my feet."

"Burrs," said Felix. "Do you remember Uncle Marvin's pigeons?"

Mei Gwen shook her head. "Uncle Marvin pulled my braids," she said. "He wanted to cut one off."

About halfway over, as they entered the tunnel on Yerba Buena Island, Mei Gwen held her nose and closed her eyes.

"Here's where the smell begins," she said.

The two men laughed. "What smell?" they asked.

"The smell of the country," said the girl.

Uncle Ed laughed a lot, told stories and made jokes, so it did not take long to get to Walnut Creek. They came to the ranch and drove out the lane to the poultry yards. There Uncle Ed's younger brother, Uncle Bob Leong, came to greet them.

Uncle Ed intended to take a truckload of poultry back to town. "Come and help me load the crates," he said.

They all got out of the truck except Mei Gwen.

"I don't like chickens," she said. "I don't want to get out."

Father looked at her. "You may stay in the truck, daughter," he said, "and observe all that goes on from there. Do not complain if you get tired of sitting still."

Mei Gwen hid her face in her hands and said nothing.

Felix went with the men. The chicken houses were enormous, each housing thousands of chickens. Felix helped chase and catch chickens and put them into the slat crates. The chickens clucked and cackled and made a great deal of noise. Feathers flew in all directions.

Mei Gwen sat in the truck with her hands over her ears, and her eyes closed. Once when she opened them, she saw a small boy of six standing near the truck, staring at her.

"Who are you?" she asked. "Are you Uncle Bob's little boy?"

"Yes, my name is Jimmy," the boy said. "I live here. What are you doing?"

"Just sitting here," said Mei Gwen.

"What is the matter?" asked Jimmy. "Can't you walk?"

"Yes, I can walk," said Mei Gwen.

"Get down and show me," said Jimmy.

Mei Gwen climbed down. It was true, she was tired of sitting still. Besides, she was getting hungry and she wanted some lunch. It must be time to eat.

Father brought a crate full of live chickens to the truck. Felix came behind with both his hands full.

"What are those black things in your hands?" asked Mei Gwen.

"Black chickens," said Felix. "See?" He held them by their legs with their heads down. "Those in that crate are black too."

"Oh, I never saw black chickens before," said Mei Gwen. "How did they get black?"

Father explained. "Chickens can be white or speckled or brown or black. Black chickens are good for sickness and fever and when your eye hurts and you cannot see well. Uncle Ed says he has many customers for them."

Felix tried to push his four black chickens into the crate.

"Do not put so many in," said Father. "They die easy, if they don't get air. Put those into the next crate."

The men brought other crates to the truck and tied them on with ropes. Then Father said it was time to eat lunch. They sat on a bench under a tree and Father opened his tea basket. The padding inside kept the tea hot for many hours. He poured the tea into paper cups and passed the sandwiches. After they had eaten, Felix went to the chicken house and came back carrying a rooster in his arms. He stroked it gently.

"See how pretty he is, Younger Sister," said Felix. "This is the father chicken. The mother chicken had red and black feathers, the father has red, black, green and yellow. These big ones eat lots of corn and other things. Uncle Bob grows all his chicken foods and feeds them every day. The father chicken is the biggest rooster in all the world. See how tame he is. Don't you want to pat him?"

"Take him away," said Mei Gwen. She would not even look.

Uncle Bob came up to her and said, "Don't you want a chicken to take home with you? I would like to give you one."

"Ugh, no!" said Mei Gwen. Then she added, politely, "No, thank you, Uncle Bob."

"She is afraid of chickens," explained Felix.

"That is because she does not know how nice they are," said Uncle Bob. "Not a big rooster like that, Felix. Take that one back to the pen. Jimmy, you go catch a young one for Mei Gwen.

It will make a nice tame pet. Then, when it gets big, she can eat it."

Jimmy ran to the nearest chicken house with his dog Terry behind him. He chased the chickens while Terry barked. He came out with a half-grown chicken in his hands. Terry was jumping up. "Terry! Don't you bite our chickens!" cried Jimmy. He took the chicken to Mei Gwen.

The girl turned away, frightened.

"I don't like it," she said. "It's got a sharp mouth . . ." She pinched her fingers together to imitate the chicken's bill. "It says all the time *gyp, gyp, gyp!*"

"This is a baby chicken," said Uncle Bob. "It will turn into a hen. In a month or two, your chicken will be twice as big as it is now. But you must feed and water it every day."

"I don't want it," wailed Mei Gwen. "It could turn into a turkey too. That turkey would fight me—it's red and black and ugly, and it's got red things hanging from its face. Aunty Rose had one and it said *turk, turk, turk* all the time."

Mei Gwen ran to Father and took his hand.

Jimmy set the chicken on the ground. It followed the girl and came near her leg. "See, it likes you," said Jimmy. Mei Gwen hid behind Father to get away from it.

Father said, "I am ashamed of you, daughter, that you are afraid of a harmless little creature like a chicken. Are you already such a city girl that you have forgotten the ways of the country? The chicken will not hurt you if you are kind to it. I will put it in your arms—gently. Just stroke it on the back as Jimmy did. I will teach you how to hold it."

Father put the chicken in the girl's arms. For one minute only. The next minute the chicken was flying across the yard and a little girl was running fast to the truck.

Father said to Felix, "Go and comfort Younger Sister."

Felix climbed up in the cab and sat down beside Mei Gwen. She leaned on his shoulder and sobbed. He listened as the words came out: "When he breathe, he go up and down in my hands. He went breathing up and down. He never sit still, he scratch me here on this arm and on both arms. He say *gyp, gyp, gyp* . . . he don't like me . . . I don't want to take Jimmy's chicken back to town with me. . . ."

Nothing more was said about a pet for Mei Gwen. When the truck drove out of the ranch gate, the tame chicken was left behind.

As the truck bounced along the highway, Felix kept thinking about Alameda. He wished Father would ask Uncle Ed to stop there. It would not be too far out of their way, and the sun was still high in the sky.

Mei Gwen leaned back on Father's shoulder and dozed. But Felix kept his eyes open. Suddenly, to his surprise, he saw a familiar street. There was the public library where he used to borrow books. There was the police station with the tall Christmas tree by the sidewalk, where Uncle Marvin used to take photographs. All the buildings were familiar.

Felix breathed deeply and his eyes sparkled. He knew that Father had asked Uncle Ed to stop at Alameda on his way back to town. His happiness was so great he could not speak. He looked at Father and smiled. Father smiled back, happy to give his eldest son an unexpected pleasure. Felix touched Mei Gwen on the arm. She opened her eyes and looked around.

"Do you know where we are, Younger Sister?" asked Felix softly.

The truck had turned off the main street into a narrow, unpaved alley. It stopped in front of a gray, unpainted frame house. A plum tree was growing in the tiny yard, its branches and foliage shading half of the raised porch. Two garage doors were below. Small houses stood in the yards on both sides and across the alley.

Mei Gwen looked around and said, "Is it *Alameda*?"

The word was magic to Felix. "Don't you *know*? Are you not *sure*? Oh, it's just the same, it hasn't changed at all!"

The children hopped down, followed by the two men. They all went up the porch steps and soon Cousin Hom and his wife

and baby came to the door and invited them in.

The first thing Father said was, "We cannot stay long. My friend, Ed Leong, must get back to the city with his poultry."

There was so much to see and so little time to see it all. Felix took Mei Gwen by the hand, led her around the house, explaining everything. Mei Gwen liked it all much better than the chicken ranch. She smiled happily as she shared Felix' enthusiasms. He showed her the plum tree by the front porch.

"It always bloomed for Chinese New Year," he said. "The blossoms were so pretty in the spring. Once Johnny Lew and I climbed up high on a branch and I didn't know it was old and it broke. I fell down with it—*kerplunk* to the ground."

"Did you hurt yourself?" asked Mei Gwen.

"My back hurt a little," said Felix. "My friends, two boys and three girls, helped me up and into the house. I told Mother and she said not to climb trees any more."

"Did you stop climbing?" asked Mei Gwen.

"No," Felix laughed. "Johnny and I climbed the cherry tree and the pear tree and the loquat tree in the back yard—" He paused. "Once we did something bad."

"What did you do?" asked Mei Gwen.

"I will start at the beginning," said Felix. "Once I saw a beautiful bird in the plum tree. It had long feathers of red and orange and purple and yellow. It looked something like that beautiful rooster I showed you today. Only it wasn't a father chicken. It must have been a magic bird—and I shot it."

"You shot it dead?" asked Mei Gwen.

"No, it didn't die," said Felix. "Johnny had his BB gun that day. He said it was a robin eating our plums. He shot first and missed it. I shot next and hit it in the wing. It fell on the ground. Then we felt sorry for it, and we took it over to Grandma Reed, the colored lady next door. She bandaged its wing to make it well. We wanted to keep it for a pet, but she said to let it go and we did. It could fly a little, sort of lopsided. We hated to see it go. After that we only shot at the plums—until Mother made us stop, because she wanted to can them. Grandma Reed thought it was a magic bird, and so do I."

"Did you ever see it again?" asked Mei Gwen.

"No," said Felix. "It never came back."

Felix took Mei Gwen around the house to the garden at the back. It was not the same, for Cousin Hom had not planted any vegetables. Grass and weeds covered the yard. Felix showed Mei Gwen just where the tomato plants grew, and the corn and the watermelons. He pointed out the cherry and pear trees, and the bamboo stalks for fishing poles. He showed her the fishpool, which was half full of water and still had two gold fish and one black fish in it. He showed her where he had buried his turtle. He told her about the fishing trips he used to take with Jack Bailey, his American friend, and Timmy Reed, the grandson of the Reeds next door.

"Mother liked it better here," Felix said. "In town she misses canning her own fruit, the pears and cherries and plums." He leaned over and picked up a caterpillar. "I used to collect caterpillars, white, gray, brown and black ones."

"Ugh! Caterpillars!" cried Mei Gwen. "Those fuzzy things! Don't put it on me!"

"I made a house for them in a coffee can," said Felix. "I put green leaves in to make them comfortable, and little sticks so they could walk up and down for exercise. I put sour-pusses in for their playmates. I fed them sugar, but I'm not sure they ate it. I think the ants did."

"Somebody's looking over the fence," said Mei Gwen.

Felix dropped the caterpillar. He looked and saw a boy's dark face staring at him. "Why, Timmy!" cried Felix. "Is that you?"

The boy climbed up on top of the fence and sat there.

"It sure is me," he said, grinning. "When did you come back, Felix? You gonna live here again like you used to?"

"No, Timmy," said Felix. "We live in San Francisco now."

"It must be nice to live in the big city," said Timmy.

"I don't like it much," said Felix.

"Well, stay here then," said Timmy, "and go fishing with me."

"I wish I could," said Felix.

The next minute Grandpa and Grandma Reed came out of their house and looked over the fence. Grandpa Reed was a little old man with white close-cropped hair, who spent most of his time reading the Bible. Grandma Reed was taller and wore a flowered silk dress and an apron. She liked to work in her garden and kept it free of weeds. They were both glad to see Felix and Mei Gwen and asked all about life in the city.

"We sure do miss you," they said.

Soon Father called from the back door. Felix and Mei Gwen had to go indoors. "Uncle Ed must start for the city," said Father.

"Can't we go to visit Uncle Marvin?" asked Felix.

"No," said Father. "It is too late."

"Where does Uncle Marvin live?" asked Mei Gwen.

"Don't you remember?" said Felix. "He has a laundry over on Central Avenue and they live upstairs. Don't you remember Aunt Lucy and the cousins, and all the pigeons in pens in his back yard?"

"Yes, I guess so," said Mei Gwen, "but it was so long ago. I was little then."

Cousin Hom's wife gave the children cakes to eat, and told them to take Chinese candies in their pockets. Soon they said goodbye and climbed back into the truck. As Uncle Ed Leong drove slowly out of the alley, a flock of pigeons flew across the sky.

"Oh, see Uncle Marvin's pigeons!" cried Felix. "How pretty they are." Then he became very quiet. He felt sad to be going away from Alameda, back to the noisy city again.

Mei Gwen dozed all the way. But that night, at home in her own bed, she could not sleep. When she did, she had a bad dream about a chicken. She dreamed it was sitting on top of her head. She said, *I shall bang him—I shall bring him back to the farm.* She threw the chicken out of the window of the apartment house, and it fell on the head of a woman walking on the sidewalk below. The woman cried out, *What shall I do? My hair is all gone. Pay me some money to buy me some more hair!*

Mei Gwen woke up crying about her bad dream. Father turned the light on and talked to her a long time before she fell asleep again.

CHAPTER IV

A Day at the Factory

Mei Gwen went running down the street, the tail of her red sweater flying behind her. A small change purse was chained to her belt. Around her neck a metal necklace kept bobbing up and down. On it hung her apartment door key and her "dog tag."

All the children in San Francisco had worn identification tags since the Second World War. The public school provided them for five cents each, and the parent provided the chain. Each tag gave the child's name and street address. Mei Gwen knew why she wore it. If she fainted on the street or got the stomach-ache, any policeman could read her tag, learn who she was and take her home. Everybody should have one.

School was out and Mei Gwen had stopped at the schoolyard, but Frankie and Freddie were not there. Where had they gone?

She ran up the steps of the apartment house. She opened the door with her key, but there was no one there. All the rooms were silent and empty. The little boys were not there and it worried her. She decided they must have gone with Felix on his paper route. Snapping the lock behind her, Mei Gwen ran down the stairs.

The girl on the second floor tried to stop her, asking, "Where are you going?" but she did not answer. She would go to the jeans factory without her brothers. They did not like it there anyhow. She ran down the Washington Street hill and crossed over Grant to Clay. It did not take long to get to Commercial Street, even though she stopped at all the red lights.

Commercial Street was not much wider than an alley, but cars came through just the same. Mei Gwen felt very much at home there. Some of the buildings had seen better days, but now were shabby and used for factories. At the lower end of the street were the well-kept offices of a label company, a printing company and a bank. Mei Gwen had made friends in all these places.

A truck was standing in front of Aunty Rose's jeans factory. The truck man had unloaded several large boxes containing blue denim cloth for making jeans and overalls. Opening a cellar door in the sidewalk, he slid the boxes down to the basement.

Mei Gwen hurried in at the front entrance. She blinked. The bright sun outside had blinded her, and the interior was very dark. The whirr of thirty-six power sewing machines and the talk and laughter of many workers made the factory a noisy place. The large room was divided by a partition. On one side the workers were mostly women, some dressed in colorful Chinese costumes, others in American dress. They started the jeans by sewing up the long side seams. On the other side of the partition, men workers sewed on pockets, belts and did the finishing details.

Aunty Rose, with a pencil behind one ear, came up holding a pile of order blanks in her hand. She was short, plump and businesslike. She ran the business, for she had a public school education, while Uncle Leon could neither read nor write, as he had had no opportunity to go to school.

"Where's Mother?" asked Mei Gwen.

Aunty Rose pointed to the back of the room. "The women want you to go to the Café and get them some coffee," she said.

Mei Gwen squeezed through the narrow aisle between the two rows of sewing machines and went to the back of the room. There,

in the darkest corner, sat Mother hard at work. She looked very small and thin, sitting before the huge sewing machine, with its shaded light throwing dark shadows across her face. Great piles of blue denim, cut into patterns, both sewed and unsewed, lay in heaps on the floor around her. This part of the room was airless, smelling of dust and lint.

"Mother!" shouted Mei Gwen.

The clatter and vibration of the roaring motors kept Mother from hearing. When she saw the girl standing there, she stopped her machine and said, "Will you go get our coffee?"

The woman at the next machine spoke up. "We want four coffees and one French toast." Several women handed the girl nickels and dimes.

"Mother," Mei Gwen began, "I couldn't find Frankie and Freddie. They were not at the schoolyard, and I stopped at the apartment and they were not there. They have run away again."

"If you see Felix," said Mother, "tell him to look for them."

"But Mother, Felix has gone on his paper route," said Mei Gwen.

"Tell him to let Roger deliver papers today," said Mother. "Tell him to look for his younger brothers. I don't want them to get lost. Felix should be responsible."

"But I won't see Felix, Mother," said Mei Gwen. "He never comes down on this street."

"Well—go get our coffee," said Mother. Then she added, "Look over there and see if Susie is still sleeping. If she's awake, take her down to the corner with you."

A door opened into a small dark room. In it there was a table, a wall sink with a water tap, and a hot plate. In the corner was a rest room with women's coats and sweaters hanging on coat hangers. Men's hats and coats hung from hooks on the side wall. On the floor, beside Aunty Rose's roll-top desk, stood a baby's playpen with a blanket draped over the sides. Inside the pen lay Susie fast asleep. Her chubby face looked flushed and she moved restlessly.

Aunty Rose was sitting at her desk. She always had business matters to take care of.

"How can Susie sleep with all this racket going on?" asked Mei Gwen.

"She has the habit," said Aunty Rose briefly. "Now run out to the Café and hurry back. Uncle Leon wants you to do some stapling in the basement."

Mei Gwen picked up a white enamel coffee pot from the table. She made her way past the men's machines to the front. Just inside the door, the factory children were playing. Cousin Paul, Aunty Rose's boy, and James Gee were wrestling, tumbling over each other on top of a pile of cardboard cartons. A red hobby-horse made a squeaking noise as little Lily Gee bounced up and down. Other small children were playing hide-and-seek among the piles of blue denim and cut-out jeans. Little Tom Chew was chasing a meowing cat.

"Take those kids outside with you, Mei Gwen," called Mrs. Gee, the mother of James and Lily, from the other side.

Mei Gwen looked at Uncle Leon. "I can't hurry if I take them," she said. "Are they all right here?"

Uncle Leon nodded. "It's O. K. as long as they stay away from the machines." He smiled. "They've got plenty places to hide in here, anyhow. You want to staple on some labels?"

"I sure do," said Mei Gwen, "just as soon as I get back."

She hurried out the door and down the street. Soon she saw a girl of her own age coming toward her. She knew who it was—Jessie Chong. She had fuzzy hair, the end of an old permanent. Jessie lived across the street from the factory. Her mother sewed for Aunty Rose, too, so Jessie was always in and out. She and all her small brothers and sisters acted as if they owned the place. One brother, Jimmy, was the meanest boy on block. He was always hitting the little children.

Mei Gwen looked at Jessie. The first thing she saw was a pile of paper tablets in Jessie's hands. Here were six or eight of them. Mei Gwen did not need to be told where they came from. There

was only one place—the Henderson Paper Company right down the street.

"Where did you get those tablets?" asked Mei Gwen.

Jessie tossed her head. "Oh, Mr. Pete Henderson gave them to me."

"I don't believe it," said Mei Gwen. "Mr. Pete gives paper only to me and to my younger brothers. Mr. Pete told me I could have all the paper I want. He told me I could take paper to my best friends or my cousins, but I was not to give it to strangers or enemies or people I don't know too well. He told me one day at lunchtime long ago, when I went to get sandwiches for my Aunty."

But Jessie Chong was very sure of herself. She smiled.

"Mr. Pete Henderson is a friend of mine too," she said. "He likes me and gives me all the paper I want. He told me to come back again whenever I want some more. He gave me enough for all my brothers and sisters."

Mei Gwen's face clouded. "I don't believe you," she said. She paused, then she added slowly and deliberately, "You stole it! He never gave it to you at all!"

Jessie Chong grew angry. She set her lips and said, "You better not say that again, Mei Gwen Fong, or I'll beat you up!"

Mei Gwen ran off down the street, holding fast to her coffee-pot. Her confidence was shattered. Had Mr. Pete really gone back on her? Mei Gwen loved her street, every inch of it. She was as much at home here in the city as Felix had been in Alameda. She knew the people who lived and worked behind every door and window. She knew and liked them all. They were not all Chinese, like up on Grant Avenue or Stockton Street. Most of them were Americans, and they treated her as if she were not Chinese at all. She was very proud of her American friends, for she felt sure they loved her.

As she passed the McClain Label Company, she looked in through the open door and saw her friend Edith. Edith was packing small boxes of labels into a large carton. Edith was tall and beautiful, with blue eyes and red hair. Edith always gave Mei Gwen scraps of silver and gold paper left over from the beautiful labels printed by the label company machines. Just to make sure that Edith was still her friend, Mei Gwen walked in.

"You still like me, don't you?" asked Mei Gwen.

"Why, of course," said Edith. "You've been my friend ever since you moved to San Francisco."

"Do you like me better than anybody else on Commercial Street?" asked Mei Gwen.

Edith thought for a minute, then she said, "I think I do." She began to look behind a counter. "Would you like . . ."

"Oh no," said Mei Gwen. "Please don't give me anything. I don't ever ask you to give me gold stars and things like that, do I?"

"Why no," said Edith. "I don't think you do."

"That's all I wanted to know," said Mei Gwen. She slipped out the door.

Her next stop was at the Henderson Paper Company. The paper company occupied the second floor over Harry's Café. Harry's Café had its entrance on Montgomery Street, but the entrance to the paper company was on Commercial. Mei Gwen had never gone up the long flight of stairs. All her dealings with Mr. Pete and Mr. John had been through their open windows.

Once long ago, when the Fongs had first moved to the city, Mei Gwen and Frankie walked down the street, lonely and sad. That day Mei Gwen saw two men upstairs at the window cutting paper with a big knife blade that went up and down like a chopper. One of the men called out to her, "You want some paper, little girl?" and Mei Gwen said, "Yes, please." They threw down some loose sheets, and she and Frankie gathered them up and took them home.

One day after that, she met the same two men in the street. They were starting to go up the stairs to the paper company. Mei Gwen spoke to them. "Are you the two gentlemans that gave me the paper?" she asked, and they said, "Yes, we are." "I just want to thank you for it," she said. She asked them their names and they told her. That was how she knew they were Mr. Pete and Mr. John.

They were the very first American friends Mei Gwen had found in the big city. They had been her friends ever since. They had given her plenty of paper—small pieces and large pieces, big pads and little pads. Every day they gave her something because they liked her. When she was baby-sitting with the factory children, she sometimes used the paper for playing school. Or, the children took pretend-rides on the cable car, and she used the paper for tickets. Mei Gwen took some of the tablets to public school. She had never run out of paper, and had never had to buy any since she had come to the city.

Now, the windows of the paper company were open, as usual.

"Hi, Mr. Pete! Hi, Mr. John!" called Mei Gwen at the top of her voice.

No one could be seen at the windows. The printing machine was making loud bangs, so she knew they were busy printing something—maybe a sign, *Apartment to Rent,* or something like that. She waited until the banging stopped and then she called again. At last Mr. John came to the window.

"No paper today," he called out. "Go away and don't bother us."

"Did you give any paper to Jessie Chong?" shouted Mei Gwen. "She wears a green sweater and has a fuzzy permanent. She's not pretty and wears glasses."

"Go away and don't bother us, I said," repeated Mr. John. He disappeared from the window.

"One thing I want to know," cried Mei Gwen loudly. "Did you give her some paper, or did she steal it?"

No answer came. The printing machine began to bang again. Mei Gwen went inside the door of the vestibule. She looked up the long flight of stairs. She wished she had courage enough to go up and find out the truth. But up at the top, she could see that the glass-fronted door with the words *Henderson Paper Company* on it was shut tight. She knew she would be too scared to open it. She called up to the window a few more times in vain.

Discouraged, she walked slowly on to Harry's Café. The women at the factory would be wanting their coffee. Maybe Jessie Chong was right. Maybe Mr. John had given the tablets to Jessie, and that's why he had none left over to give to Mei Gwen. Mei Gwen felt very sad.

As soon as she went inside the Café, she felt better for she knew she was among friends again. Mr. Harry was always nice to her and she adored his waitresses. There were three, Dorothy and Tootsie and a new one. Mei Gwen liked Tootsie the best. Tootsie gave her a paint set last year for Christmas and Mr. Harry gave her a plastic doll for her birthday, a doll that opened and shut its eyes.

The waitresses were busy serving office people sitting on stools at the large circular counter. Mr. Harry was cashier, but he stopped work and took Mei Gwen's coffeepot and shouted her order to the kitchen at the back, "Four coffees and one French toast to go." Soon he came forward with the pot full of coffee and a paper sack in his hands.

Mei Gwen studied the new waitress. She had bunchy black hair in loose curls on her shoulders. She had white ivory-ball earrings bobbing in her ears. Her eyebrows were thin, sharp black lines, and her lips were painted red with lipstick.

"Gee! I don't like her," Mei Gwen whispered to Tootsie, who had blue eyes and bleached blonde hair. "She looks like some kind of a bird to me. What's her name?"

"Beverly," said Tootsie. "She used to be an actress."

"Whew!" said Mei Gwen. "In the movies? Maybe I'll like her after all."

"Here's an orange for you," said Tootsie, slipping it into the girl's pocket. "Now see that you don't spill that hot coffee and scald yourself."

Mei Gwen paid Mr. Harry the money in her hand and picked up the pot.

Mr. Harry smiled and said, "Mei Gwen knows how to carry it. She has learned to stuff the spout with a paper napkin to keep it from spilling. She holds the pot with napkins so she won't burn her hand."

A man held the door open and Mei Gwen walked out. She went past the doors of the paper company and the label company without stopping. When she reached the factory, the little children were playing on the sidewalk by the door. They danced around Mei Gwen and began teasing her.

"Tell us a story! Tell us about the polar bear!" cried Cousin Jean. "Take us for a walk," begged James and Lily Gee. "Let's play marching!" said Larry. "No, I want to sing *Mulberry Bush*," cried little Dorinda, jumping up and down.

It made Mei Gwen happy to see how much the little children liked her. It was fun to be a baby sitter. She never ran out of ideas and the little ones always minded her. She happened to look up, and there across the street, standing at the second story apartment house window, she saw Jessie Chong as big as life. Jessie had a large tablet in one hand and a big red pencil in the other. She was busy writing on the tablet. She held it up so Mei Gwen could be sure to see.

Mei Gwen turned quickly and went in. "Get away," she said to the little ones, "before I spill hot coffee on you."

Back in the rear of the factory, the women who had ordered coffee stopped work and drank. All the work was piecework, each worker being paid for the number of pieces sewed, so they could stop whenever they wished. Only Aunty Rose was cross.

"Why did you stay so long?" she asked. "Uncle Leon is tired of waiting for you. You are big enough to do a little work and not play all day long."

The little ones tried to get Mei Gwen to come and play with them, but Aunty Rose shooed them out on the sidewalk.

"Don't go on the street, or the trucks will run over you," called Aunty Rose. "Don't run away or the policemens will catch you."

Mei Gwen went down to the basement.

The cutting and finishing of the jeans was done in the basement. On one side were two cutting tables half a block long. Uncle Leon and a man helper were busy cutting. The electric cutting machines followed stencil patterns marked on the cloth. They cut through six or seven dozen thicknesses of blue denim in one operation—a pile five inches thick. Enough pieces had already been cut to keep the workers busy sewing through the coming week.

In the other half of the basement, hundreds of piles of jeans and overalls lay on floor and tables. Two young women were working at pressing machines, which pressed pocket pieces and turned the edges under. The other workers were Chinese grandmothers, little old wrinkled women dressed in long straight black Chinese gowns, with their hair knotted in little buns on their necks. One of them was Grandmother Yee. Mei Gwen found a place beside her and picked up scissors and stapler.

"Now I have a helper," said Grandmother with a smile. "These are the cowboy labels for this stack. Cut the threads off and staple the labels on. I'll fold them and put them in bundles of twelve."

"Just think, Grandmother," said Mei Gwen, "real cowboys will be wearing these jeans while they ride and jump around on their horses. I saw them in the movies and their jeans looked just like these." She picked them up and snipped off loose threads, then stapled a label on one pocket of each pair.

"So I see," said Grandmother, studying the picture of a bucking bronco on the colorful label.

"And boys and girls all over the United States will be wearing them too—these small sizes," Mei Gwen went on. "Uncle Leon says all the small sizes are worn by boys and girls. It doesn't matter if they are rich or poor, or live in the country or the city. It is the style now for everybody to wear blue jeans!"

Grandmother shook her head. It was hard for her to get used to the strange ways of a new country.

When Uncle Leon finished his cutting job, he came over to the bundle table. As the old women bundled the jeans, he sent the bundles up to the first floor on a moving belt. Uncle Leon was very proud of the moving belt. It had cost him four hundred dollars and he liked to brag about it. "Boy!" he said, "am I glad I bought that! My back doesn't ache any more now. When I used to carry all those bundles up the stairs, it was hard on my back and my legs too."

The afternoon passed quickly. Soon it was time for the workers to go home. Mother and Mei Gwen and baby Susie walked part way with Grandmother Yee. She lived only three blocks from the factory, in a small apartment with Aunty Kate and Uncle Fred. Downstairs Aunty Kate had a beauty parlor which kept her busy.

On the way home, Mei Gwen kept looking for Frankie and Freddie. Mother insisted on walking through Portsmouth Square. But there was no sign of the two little boys on the swings or the slides, and the benches were filled with old men with hats on. Mei Gwen and her mother stopped at the Lotus Garden Restaurant, but Father had not seen the boys and they were not at home when Mei Gwen got there.

It was nearly eight o'clock when Felix, tired and hungry, came back from Chinese school. Father met him at the door.

"Where are your younger brothers?" he asked.

"I don't know," said Felix. "I went on my paper route with Roger Loy. . . ."

"Go and look for your younger brothers," said Father sternly. "Do not return until you have found them. You should know by this time that they are your responsibility."

An hour later Felix returned, holding Frankie tightly by one hand and Freddie by the other.

"Where were they?" demanded Father.

"Hiding in the playground on Sacramento Street," said Felix. "They made me hunt and hunt for them. At last I heard them laughing. I looked up and there they were, hiding in the branches of that big tree by the gate. They said they were pigeons learning to fly. They held their arms out like wings, but they were afraid to jump. They were happy because they had found a tree to climb in San Francisco."

Frankie and Freddie had been standing silent, hanging their heads. Now they began to giggle. But when the saw the stick in Father's hand, they stopped. After they were punished, they promised not to run away again.

CHAPTER V

The Lost Dog

Felix stood by the high brick wall on the roof of the apartment house. He could see boats coming and going in San Francisco Bay. His eye could follow the Bay bridge over to Yerba Buena Island and beyond, where the shore line melted in a blue haze. If only he had a telescope, he could see all the way to Alameda. Maybe he could even see Uncle Marvin's pigeons flying.

"*Frankie!* Get *down!*"

Mei Gwen's loud scream woke Felix up from his daydreaming.

He turned and looked across the roof to the street side. There was Frankie, stepping on a box, climbing to the top of the wall, in danger of toppling over. The next minute, Mei Gwen had pulled him down.

"Did you see him? Did you see that man down on the street?" cried Frankie.

"What did you do, Younger Brother?" asked Mei Gwen sternly.

"I threw a comic book down on his head." Frankie laughed. "He didn't know where it came from!"

"You are not to get up on that wall," said Mei Gwen. "If you fell down into the street, it would not be funny at all."

"It is well you threw the comic book away," said Felix. "Father says he will not have that trash in our house. If he catches us reading one, he will punish us."

It was warm up on the apartment house roof in spite of the wind. The roof was the next best thing to a real yard, and the children liked to play there. The boys could run and jump around, except when the Yicks in Apartment No. 7 below complained.

There were chimneys and skylights and water tanks on the roof. There were clotheslines where Mother hung her clothes to dry. There were radio and television antennae.

In one corner of a small fenced-in yard, Father had several salted fish hanging on a line to dry. Baskets of shrimp and other seafood were spread out in the sun. Behind the chimney Mei Gwen had a dollhouse made from a cardboard carton. Father had told her to give her dolls to Susie and Grandmother said she was too old to play with them. So she kept them hidden up on the roof. Now she got them out and began to play.

Suddenly a girl came up the stairs from below. It was the girl from Apartment No. 3. Her hair was uncombed and she was not very clean. She had a little brother and sister behind her.

"My name is Sandra Sung," she said. "What's yours?"

Mei Gwen looked at the girl's dirty dress.

"How many dolls you got?" asked Sandra.

Mei Gwen did not answer the question.

"If your father runs a laundry," she said sternly, "why don't you wear clean dresses?"

The girl's eyes filled with tears. She took her brother and sister by the hand and went back down the stairs.

Then Mother Fong came. "Why is that little girl crying?" she asked. "You didn't hurt her, did you, daughter?"

"No, Mother," said Mei Gwen, but she felt ashamed inside.

Mother called Frankie and Freddie, and they helped her bring up a basket of wet clothes, ready to hang on the line. Seeing Felix standing alone, looking so sadly across the water, Mother went over to him. She spoke softly so the others could not hear.

"You must not grieve so much, my son," she said. "Only time will ease the pain of homesickness. All of us who were born in the old country have felt it, too."

Felix made no sign that he heard her words. His lip quivered—that was all.

Aloud, Mother said, "Go to the grocery store, my son, and get me a box of soap powder." She handed him some money. "I still have all the blue jeans and shirts of Father and my three boys to wash. They will make another washer full."

Felix turned and went slowly down the steps.

Did Mother really want soap powder, or did she just want him to go for a walk? Felix was not sure. There were grocery stores in almost every block, but he just kept on walking. He would take a walk anyhow, and pick up the soap powder on his way back.

Just then a cable car came clanging along Mason Street from Fisherman's Wharf. They had seemed strange to the boy at first—these little open trolley cars carried along by an underground cable that clicked and rattled in the little ditch between the two rails. But Felix was used to them now. Once he rode on one to Market Street with Mother, and once Father took the whole family to Golden Gate Park for a picnic on a Sunday afternoon.

How about a ride? Felix had money of his own in his pocket, so he got on at Jackson Street. At Washington, the cable car turned south to Powell. Near the corner, the grip man released the grip on the cable and let the car coast, shouting, "Look out for the curve!" The passengers held on tight as the car shot around. When it stopped at Sacramento, Felix jumped off.

He walked down Sacramento Street. The hill was so steep that

traffic was one-way and cars were parked going up only. People could go both ways on the sidewalk, but it was hard to walk up the hill on windy days.

Hearing shouts, Felix looked behind him. Two boys were coming down on a new kind of scooter. They had been to the library, and each boy had placed his library book on a single roller skate, and was sitting on it, with knees bent up in front of him. Felix stepped out of the way, laughing. What fun to do that! He knew the boys, too. They were in his class at school—Ronnie Chow and Ralph Hom. They rolled on past him, gathering speed as they went.

Then all at once, another boy came zooming from behind on a soap-box scooter. Felix heard him coming and jumped out of his way. It was Sammy Hong and he whistled like a diesel engine to let people know he was coming. At Stockton Street, the three boys waited for a green light and crossed over. Felix followed them to the playground.

Sometimes when Roger was there they let him play, for they knew he was Roger's partner. But Roger was taking the paper route today, so Felix knew he would not be there, but perhaps they would let him play just the same.

When he came in, Ronnie and Ralph and Sammy were throwing a basketball. Sammy tossed it to Felix, shouting, "There, Dumbo, see if you can catch it!" It was unexpected and Felix was not ready for the ball, so it landed on the back of his neck and bounced off. Ralph Hom caught it and threw it back to Sammy. The boys began to call Felix names—Sap and Dumbo and Dopey. It was no use—Felix walked away and sat down on a bench.

It was then that he saw the dog come running into the playground. It was a small dog with long light brown hair and floppy ears and short tail. The boys teased the dog with sticks. They chased it, saying, "Get out of here. We want to play our game." The dog ran into the street and Felix ran after it. It came to him when he called. He sat on the curbstone and patted it.

"What's your name, doggie?" he asked. "Where is your home? Are you lost in the big city?"

The dog wagged his tail and looked at Felix with his big brown eyes. *Oh, if I could only keep him,* thought Felix, *how happy I would be. I would not mind living in the city, if I had a dog of my own.* He held the dog in his arms, and it seemed contented there.

"That's not *your* dog," someone said.

Felix looked up. Sammy Hong was standing near, leaning on his scooter.

"I know he isn't," said Felix, "but I like him."

"He's got a collar with a tag on it," said Sammy. "That means he belongs to somebody."

"If I can find the owner," said Felix, "I'll give the dog back to him. But if I can't, I'll keep him myself."

"Take him to the police station," said Sammy. "They'll find the owner for you."

"Where's that?" asked Felix. "Where should I go?"

Sammy told him where the police station was, then he whizzed off down the street on his scooter.

Felix thought about it for a while. He wished he could see Policeman Mike and ask him about it, but the policeman was nowhere in sight. Felix wondered who the owner could be. Maybe the dog was homesick for his master. There was only one thing to do—take him to the police station.

It was a long walk down to lower Washington Street. Felix carried the dog across the streets, then let it walk on the sidewalks at his heels. The police station was next door to the morgue, the prison and the Hall of Justice. Felix was timid, not knowing where to go. Police cars and ambulances were coming and going, and once a police siren went off. The noise hurt the dog's ears and he howled. Felix saw an open door and went in, with the dog following close behind. A policeman sitting at a desk asked him what he wanted.

"I found a lost dog . . ." began Felix.

The policeman got up and started toward the door. When the

dog saw him coming, he barked at him and would not let him pass.

"Take your dog and get out of here," said the policeman gruffly. "Go to the office round the corner."

Felix grabbed the dog hastily and went out. In the next office there were five policemen, all talking about robbers and thieves. They looked at the boy and listened to his story, but they said they had no time for lost dogs.

Felix went out feeling very sad. He put the dog down on the sidewalk. Should he go to the Lotus Garden Restaurant and ask Father what to do? Father would put the dog outside the door and make Felix stay and wash dishes for a while. No, he did not want to go there. Back up Washington Street he went, then up the hill again to the playground. Maybe by this time the dog's owner would be there looking for him.

On the corner he saw Policeman Mike, the friend of all the school children. Felix told him his story and showed him the dog. Policeman Mike patted Felix on the shoulder and said, "Why don't you keep him, sonny?"

"But if he's homesick . . ." began the boy.

Felix went into the playground and sat on a bench. The boys saw the dog and began teasing him again. They threw balls at the dog to see if he could catch them. They threw sticks and tried to get the dog to bring the sticks back. They kept the dog running in circles and barking loudly.

The dog was yelping so, Felix knew he was unhappy. He picked him up and went out the gate, starting for home. He carried him all the way to the apartment. He began to hope he would never find the owner. Then he could keep the dog himself.

Would Mother let him keep a dog in the crowded apartment? What would Father say? Would he approve of having a pet in the city?

The dog ran all the way up the three flights of stairs. He followed Felix and came when he called. At the top, the door stood open and there was Mei Gwen.

"Did you bring the soap powder?" she asked. "Mother has been waiting hours for it."

"No, I forgot about it," said Felix. "I found a dog. Look what a nice little dog I found."

Mei Gwen remembered the barking dog called Terry at the Walnut Creek ranch. "A dog!" she cried. "What do you want a dog for?"

"Of course it's not my dog," said Felix. "I suppose it belongs to somebody."

Hearing voices, Mother and little Susie came to the front room. Mother asked for the soap powder. Maybe she really needed it after all. Felix had to explain all over again. Little Susie put her arms around the dog's neck. The dog stood very still while she patted him on the head.

"He likes Susie," said Felix.

"Have you looked at his dog tag?" asked Mother.

Felix looked at the tag dangling from the dog's collar. "It's got his license number," he said. He turned the tag over. "It says, 'If this dog is lost or injured, please phone Market 11701 for name and address of owner.' "

"That must be the dog pound, the place where they keep lost dogs," said Mother. "You should telephone that number."

"I don't want to," said Felix. Deep in his heart, he did not care to find the owner, because he wanted to keep the dog.

"You must find the owner quickly," said Mother. "When a dog gets homesick, it will not eat or drink. It will die."

"I will feed him," said Felix. "What does a dog eat?"

"Dog food," said Mei Gwen promptly. "I have seen it at the Fat Lung Grocery. They sell it in tin cans. All the cans have pictures of dogs on them."

"I have my own money," said Felix, looking at his mother. "I will buy him dog food. I will buy you the soap powder too."

"Let me go with you," said Mei Gwen.

Mother said nothing, so the children started out. The dog followed them to the store and back again. Mei Gwen gave the soap powder to Mother. Felix opened the can of dog food with a can opener and smelled it.

"My dog will like this," he said. "It smells something like pressed ham."

Felix put some of the food on a dish. He set the dish on a newspaper on the floor. Mei Gwen brought a pan of water. The dog ate and drank. Felix was happy because now he knew the dog was not homesick.

Mother came down from the roof, bringing some of the clothes that were dry. She asked, "Have you telephoned the dog pound?"

"No, Mother," said Felix. "The dog likes it here. He is not going to die of homesickness. See how he eats! I will spend all my paper route money to buy him good food."

Mother spoke crossly, "Mei Gwen, what was that number on the dog's tag? Go to the telephone and call it. Find out who owns this dog, so he may be restored to his owner." She turned to Felix. "When a dog is lost, it is a kindness to restore it to the owner. If you try to keep a lost dog, it is the same as stealing it."

Felix' heart sank. Now he knew—there was only one thing to do. It was a hard thing to do, because already he loved the little dog so much. *I would like to keep him if the owner did not want him,* he thought. *Maybe the owner will say that he does not want him—then he will be mine.* But Felix knew this was a foolish hope.

"I will take him for a little walk on the street, Younger Sister," said Felix, "while you do the telephoning."

Felix hated the telephone. He could never get used to it—talking into a little black thing sitting on the bookcase. Father never had a telephone in Alameda, because he had no use for such a thing. When he wanted to talk to people, he went to see them and talked to them face to face. Felix did not like the idea of talking to people you could not see. But Mei Gwen liked it, as she liked all city ways. She was always telephoning her girl-friends and having long visits with them, until Mother made her hang up.

Mei Gwen did the telephoning. She called Market 11701 and a lady said, "This is the S. P. C. A."

"What's that?" asked Mei Gwen.

The lady explained that it was the Society for the Prevention of Cruelty to Animals. Mei Gwen gave the dog's license number, and the lady told her the owner's name and address. Mei Gwen looked up the owner's number in the telephone book. She called the number and a man answered. She asked him if he had lost his dog and he said yes.

Meanwhile Felix sat in the downstairs doorway and held the dog on his knees. At first he thought of saving the dog by running away with him. But where could he go to keep the dog safe? Then he remembered his mother's words. He patted the dog and talked to him.

"I am trying to bring you back to your master as fast as I can," he said. He told the dog this, so he would understand. He wanted the dog to know he was trying to help him.

A man came walking down the street. He was an old, old Chinese man with a stick across his shoulder. Tied to the stick were chairs, two hanging in front and two in back, a heavy load. He was taking them to the chair factory for repairs.

The man was a stranger to Felix and to the dog. The unusual sight frightened the dog. He jumped up and down and barked at the old man, who turned around in anger and spoke to Felix in Chinese.

"Who is your unfortunate father," he said, "who has not properly instructed his son to show respect to his elders?"

Felix bowed his head, ashamed. Then he spoke.

"Please, grandfather, would you please walk on the other side of the street?" he asked timidly. "This little dog is lost. That is why he is barking so loudly."

Felix could not catch the dog because he kept on jumping and barking. A Negro man carrying a live chicken walked by. The little dog forgot the chair man and barked at the Negro.

"Please, mister," begged Felix, "would you mind walking on the other side of the street, so I can catch my dog?"

"I'll catch him for you—by the tail!" said the man, chasing the

dog. The dog ran in circles and barked still more.

When the dog barked, it frightened Felix. The dog made such a loud noise, and Felix did not know how to stop it. He was afraid a policeman might come and take the dog away from him, thinking he did not know how to care for it properly.

A young man came along, carrying a tray of food on his head. He came from the restaurant down the street and was delivering a hot meal to somebody's apartment. The dog barked again, but this time Felix held him tight in his arms and he soon stopped.

Just then Mei Gwen came to the front door and called. Felix went over to her. "He's coming," she said.

"Who?" asked Felix.

"The owner," said Mei Gwen. "The man said, 'Wait half an hour and I'll be there.' "

"Did you tell him where we live?" asked Felix.

"Yes," said Mei Gwen.

"Oh, why did you do that?" groaned Felix.

"So he can come and get his dog," said Mei Gwen. "The dog's name is Rusty, he said."

" 'Rusty'—I like that name," said Felix. "Did he sound like a nice man—like a kind man?"

"He was O.K.," said Mei Gwen.

"Where does he live?" asked Felix unhappily.

"Up on Nob Hill," said Mei Gwen. "The man said that when he took his car out of the garage this morning, he forgot to close the door, so the dog ran away."

"The dog was happy," said Felix, "because he was free. Maybe he felt like Frankie and Freddie when they run away. They don't like to be cooped up in a little crowded apartment. The dog did not like to be locked in the man's garage. That is why he ran away. To run away does not always mean that one is bad. Maybe it just means a person is unhappy. A dog could be unhappy, too. Maybe the man does not treat him well."

Mei Gwen and Felix sat in the doorway and talked. The dog lay contentedly in Felix' arms. Sandra Sung, the girl from the second-floor apartment, came out and stood on the sidewalk. She looked shabby, but she had put on a clean dress.

"Oh, you've got a dog," she said.

It seemed no time at all before a taxi pulled up and an American man stepped out. He called, "Here, Rusty!" The dog heard it and jumped up and down, he was so glad to see his master. He barked a little, too—happy barks, not angry barks. The man wanted the dog back. There was no use Felix asking if he could keep him. The man talked to the children, but Felix did not hear a word he said. Mei Gwen answered all the man's questions. She was not afraid of Americans and strangers.

The man put a leash on the dog's collar. The dog stood still and let him snap it on. That settled the matter. The dog was willing to go back to his master.

Felix and Mei Gwen said goodbye to the dog. Felix' voice was shaking. He hated to see the dog go away. The man got into the taxi and the dog jumped in after him. The taxi drove off down the street and turned the corner. The dog was gone.

Standing there, Felix looked down and saw that he held a dollar bill in his hand.

"Where did I get this?" he asked, astonished.

"The man gave it to you, Elder Brother," said Mei Gwen. "He said it was your reward."

"Did he?" asked Felix.

What was it—the motto in the Fortune cookie? *Better to keep a friend than to have a dollar.* In his mind, Felix changed it: *Better to keep a dog than to have a dollar.* No amount of money could make up for the loss of the dog.

"Here, Younger Sister," said Felix. "You can have the dollar."

"Oh, thank you," said Mei Gwen.

She took the money and ran up the stairs.

CHAPTER VI

A Day for Growing Up

"Today is an important day," said Mei Gwen.

Grandmother Yee, who had come early that morning, said, "Each day is important if we make it so."

"But today is my birthday," said Mei Gwen. "I am ten years old."

"I hope you are also ten years wise," said Grandmother. "You will have to help me get things ready for tonight."

"It is to be a party?" asked Mei Gwen.

"All the family are coming," said Grandmother, "and you may ask some of the neighbors. There will be much to do before Mother comes home from the factory."

"I will help all I can," said Mei Gwen.

Grandmother ordered the chicken on the telephone. Then she said, "Take this shopping bag and go to the Sang Sang Poultry

Shop and get the chicken. Uncle Ed will have it ready for you. I ordered a nice plump one, four and a half pounds. I will fix it in a special way for tonight."

"But I don't like to go," said Mei Gwen.

"No?" said Grandmother. "Why not?"

"I am scared of chickens," said Mei Gwen. "They have sharp things for a mouth. They bite you. They say *gyp-gyp-gyp* all the time."

Grandmother laughed. "You talk like a city girl."

"I have been to the country and I *know*," said Mei Gwen. "I have seen them alive. I know how they breathe up and down and I have heard all the noise they make. Father took us with Uncle Ed to his brother's chicken ranch. Uncle Ed brings them all alive to his poultry shop. He has them all over the sidewalk and piled up in boxes inside. I do not like to go there."

"No?" said Grandmother. "That is too bad. Without a chicken we cannot have a nice birthday for you."

Mei Gwen became silent, thinking fast.

"The chicken will be all ready?" she asked. "Are you sure?"

Grandmother nodded. "So he said."

"Uncle Ed will just have to put it in my shopping bag—that is all?" asked Mei Gwen.

"That is all," said Grandmother, smiling.

"Maybe that won't be so bad," said the girl.

"To be a good housewife," said Grandmother, "you must always buy your chickens fresh. Uncle Ed brings them in from the country alive, so his customers can be sure to get them freshly killed. A fresh chicken always tastes better and is more nourishing, too. It makes people strong and healthy."

Grandmother put a small package in the girl's hands.

"I have saved all our left-over cooked rice and dried it," she said. "Take it to our friend, Ed Leong, to feed to his ducks and chickens."

"But Grandmother, nobody else does that," said Mei Gwen. "Nobody else saves rice to feed somebody's old fat chickens."

"Rice is so hard to come by, we must not waste a single grain," said Grandmother. "Some one had to work hard to grow that rice. Don't ever waste food. The Creator gives each person only so much food. If you waste it or use up your share too quickly, you will be sure to starve."

Mei Gwen put the rice in her shopping bag and got ready to go.

"I must pass the Yet Sang Fish Shop," she said to herself. "So I will wear my old yellow sweater." She put it on over her blue blouse. She fastened her change purse to her belt. She made sure she was wearing her necklace with her door key and identification tag.

"Stop at the Fung Wo grocery for the greens and vegetables," said Grandmother. "Mr. Sue will have them ready for you."

Mei Gwen felt very important to do the day's shopping alone, without Grandmother. She felt like a real housewife. On the street she saw several Chinese grandmothers with shopping bags. They were shopping for their married daughters, who were working at jobs in the factories or were kept at home with small children. Each week, under Grandmother's careful guidance, Mei Gwen was learning more and more about housekeeping. She knew which vegetables were fresh and which a day old. She knew the names of the dried seafoods in all the many baskets across the front of the Fung Wo Grocery.

When she got there, Mr. Sue had everything ready. He put her vegetables in a paper bag and handed it to her. He spoke in a businesslike way and called her by name. Mei Gwen liked buying vegetables for Grandmother, but there was one thing she did not like. That was buying a live chicken.

But she told herself, this time it would be easy. Uncle Ed would have it ready, it would be all wrapped in paper so she need not even look at it. He could pop it into her shopping bag and off she

would go. That was all there was to it. She marched along confidently.

She stopped in front of the Yet Sang Fish Shop to look at the turtles and the frogs. The turtles were fast asleep, but the frogs were jumping. Not one of them sat still to stare at a little girl passing by. Not one of them noticed her old yellow sweater. She felt a little cheated, somehow.

Mei Gwen could tell when she was coming near the poultry shop. She heard the squawks of the chickens while she was still half a block away. There was Uncle Ed Leong on the back of the truck unloading crates. One crate fell down, the door came open and out came the chickens, very much alive. They ran and jumped and flew in all directions. Boys and men on the sidewalk ran after the chickens. They caught them and put them back in the crate. One young rooster led them a merry chase. It came toward Mei Gwen and she drew back hastily. It flew up on the awning of the Yet Sang Fish Shop and roosted there. Mr. Lum, the fish man, came out with a fish net on a long pole, crept up quickly and caught the rooster. He gave it to Uncle Leong, who took it inside.

"Oh dear!" said Mei Gwen. "I hope Uncle Ed will not keep me waiting. I want to get away from here quickly. I do not like this neighborhood."

The poultry truck moved away and the sidewalk grew calm. Mei Gwen approached cautiously. Seeing no stray chickens, she walked up to the shop and went in.

Uncle Ed Leong sat at a very neat desk at the back of the room. On one side a counter was piled high with fifty-pound sacks of Texas rice for sale. Along the other side was a long counter with

chicken crates below it. Across the top were hooks from which dressed chickens were hanging. Nearby was a large scale for weighing. A loose end of string hung down from a large ball fastened to the wall. A pile of newspapers lay beside the cash register.

In the open rooms beyond, Mei Gwen could see three men working busily. She could also hear all the noise the chickens were making. She was glad they were all in cages. The crates and cages lined the walls from floor to ceiling. Some chickens were saying *gyp-gyp-gyp* and some were going *cluck, cluck, cluck,* and some were making a loud squawking. Mei Gwen wanted to put her hands over her ears, but she had to hold her nose because she did not like the smell.

She went up to Mr. Leong at his desk. He had an abacus in his hand and was busy counting. The abacus was a beautifully made oblong wooden frame, with wires stretched up and down, on which were strung rows of wooden beads. It was an age-old adding machine for doing accounts. Mr. Leong moved the beads up and down, making soft sounds with his lips. On the desk in front of him, in a neat pile, lay his Chinese account books. A small tray held his writing brush, ink box and seals. Sometimes he stopped and wrote in his books.

Mei Gwen waited patiently until he looked up at her.

"Ah! the little girl of my friend, Frank Fong!" said Uncle Ed. "I am glad to see you this beautiful morning."

Mei Gwen took the small package from her shopping bag. "My Grandmother Yee sends you this dried rice, Uncle Ed, to feed your chickens," she said. "My Grandmother Yee saves all the left-over rice at our house and dries it."

Mr. Leong took the package and thanked the girl. "Your honorable Grandmother is a thrifty woman," he said. "It is very kind of her to remember my unworthy chickens."

"My chicken—is it ready?" asked Mei Gwen timidly.

"*Your* chicken?" asked Mr. Leong.

"It is for my birthday," said Mei Gwen modestly. "My Grandmother Yee ordered it over the telephone. You said it would be ready for me to take home when I came."

Mr. Leong became businesslike at once. "The hen will be ready in a minute, young lady," he said. "I will take care of it myself to see that the daughter of my friend, Frank Fong, is properly served." He went to the back of the room where most of the crates were. "How many pounds does she want—four? five?"

"But my chicken is all ready, Uncle Ed," said Mei Gwen. "You do not need to kill another one. My Grandmother told me not to wait."

Mr. Leong came forward again. He placed a chair in front of his desk. He brought copies of *Life* and *Look* magazines.

"Come, sit down and be comfortable, young lady," he said. "Why should you be in a hurry? You have all the time there is. You do not want to rush around madly as these Americans do. Go slow, take your time, meditate more and you will live longer—that is the Chinese philosophy. I want the little daughter of my good friend, Frank Fong, to suffer no inconvenience. You like to read, eh? You are a smart girl in the public school, eh? And in Chinese evening school, too? You get the highest marks in the class?"

Mei Gwen did not look up at him. She sat down on the chair. She took the magazines on her lap, but she did not open them. How could she bear to live through it? How could she keep from running away? What did it matter whether she had a chicken for her birthday or not? She hated chickens and never wanted to see one again. The chicken was not ready at all.

But she sat there on her chair and did not move. She knew

what was going on, although she never once looked up.

Mr. Leong picked a plump live chicken from the cage and weighed it on the scales. He grabbed the chicken by its legs, twisted the legs so it could not get away, then he made a sharp cut in its neck. As the chicken fluttered, he stuck it into a large garbage can and put the cover down tight. Quickly Mei Gwen put her hands over her ears, so she would not hear it say *gubble-gubble-gub.* She did not want to hear it jumping inside the can. This was the worst part and she was glad when it was over.

Mr. Leong pulled his sleeves up and took the chicken out of the

can. He dipped it into a large open tank filled with boiling water. He pressed a pedal with his foot and held it up to a machine that pulled the feathers off. The machine was run by electricity. It was a revolving drum with rubber spikes on it. It was like a wild wind and made a roaring noise. It pulled the feathers off and they fell in a box on the floor.

The chicken was now ready to be dressed. Uncle Ed washed it carefully at the sink, cleaned all the pin feathers off, and chopped it into small pieces, discarding the entrails. Finally, after what seemed a long time to a small girl, he plopped a heavy newspaper-wrapped package into Mei Gwen's shopping bag. He kept her waiting still longer by the door, as he inquired after all the members of the Fong family, and listened while Mei Gwen reported them well and happy.

When Mei Gwen came out of the poultry store, she saw three girls playing *Shake, shake, shake* on the sidewalk. Gaily they chanted:

"Shake, shake, shake,
Oh playmate,
Come out and play with me
And bring your dolly sweet
And eat your apple treat."

They joined hands and shook three times. Then they clapped, hitting opposing hands, and with a light tap on the leg, whirled around. Two of the girls were classmates at school, Linda Lee and Ethel Wong. The third, an American, Mei Gwen had not seen before.

"Now we'll teach you a Chinese game," they said. Linda and Ethel began:

> "Chong chong dō,
> High go show,
> To my row,
> Chong chong go."

They explained the gestures which ended the verse. "Two fingers means *scissors,*" said Linda. "The closed fist means *a rock,* and the open hand means *paper.*"

"When two players make the same gesture," said Ethel, "that means the other one is *out.*"

They started playing again, but the new girl did not seem to understand the game.

"I can explain it better than you can," said Mei Gwen.

"Who do you think you are?" said Ethel.

"Nobody asked you to play," said Linda.

They looked Mei Gwen up and down. Then Ethel took Linda by the arm and they walked off down the street. The American girl was left alone with Mei Gwen, who asked her her name.

"Dina Costelli," said the girl.

In a few minutes, Mei Gwen learned all about her. Her father ran the Italian Market down the street in the next block. She lived in Little Italy, not far from Chinatown. She said she liked Chinese girls. She walked all the way home with Mei Gwen, so she could see where she lived. Before they parted, Dina had promised to be Mei Gwen's girl-friend and to come to her birthday party that evening.

Grandmother Yee said nothing when Mei Gwen came in, but started to prepare the chicken at once. Mei Gwen ran down the steps of the apartment house to knock at the doors and invite her neighbors. She invited Lester Yang on the third floor and Mrs. Ping and her baby. The Quans on the second floor were not at home, but Sandra Sung, the untidy little girl, was sitting on the steps as usual, and her little brother and sister were crying inside. Mei Gwen passed her without speaking. Down on the first floor, she invited old Mr. Wong. He said he would come and bring his Chinese butterfly harp.

Upstairs again, she invited Mrs. Yick and Ellen and Elaine, the five-year-old twins across the hall. The twins came over and helped Mei Gwen set the table. Soon Mother returned from the factory with the younger boys and little Susie. Mother was surprised to see how much had been done. Things began to happen quickly after that.

Mother brought large boxes with her, and when Mei Gwen opened them, she had a grand surprise. There were a new blue birthday dress, new shoes and socks and new ribbons for Mei Gwen's hair. Mother said she could put them on and wear them. So a pretty Mei Gwen opened the door each time the doorbell rang.

"Is she coming? Is she coming?" Mei Gwen kept asking. She was thinking of her new friend, Dina Costelli.

The first time she went to the door it was Aunty Rose Jong with her children, Paul, Dorinda and Jean. The next time it was Father, home early from the restaurant. He had stopped at a bakery and bought a large birthday cake. He decorated it with candles and set it in the middle of the table. The other relatives and the neighbors from downstairs came in one after the other. Old Mr. Wong brought his butterfly harp, sat in the corner and played Chinese music. Two friends of Father's came and sang Chinese songs. It was nearly eight when Felix got back from Chinese school. Mei Gwen was glad to see everybody, but she felt a little sad that Dina Costelli, her new-found friend, did not appear.

At last dinner was ready and they all sat down to eat. Besides the chicken which was simmered in soy sauce, there were other delicious dishes—steamed prawns with black bean sauce, bird's-nest soup and barbecued pork. The table was big and round and they could all reach the dishes in the center with their chopsticks. Friends and family talked and laughed merrily. Suddenly the doorbell rang and Mei Gwen jumped up.

"I know who it is," she said. "It's my new girl-friend."

She ran down the hall to open the door.

What was her surprise to see not Dina Costelli from Little Italy, but Sandra Sung, the laundryman's little girl from the second floor.

"What do *you* want?" asked Mei Gwen sharply.

She was ready to close the door in the girl's face, but she looked at her again. Sandra's face was clean, her hair nicely brushed, and she had on a brand-new dress. Mei Gwen looked at her twice. Sandra Sung's dress was a nylon party dress, exactly like Mei Gwen's own, except that it was pink instead of blue.

"I came to your birthday party," said Sandra.

"But I didn't invite you!" said Mei Gwen.

"Your mother did . . ." cried Sandra, tears coming to her eyes.

"Bring her in!" called Father from the kitchen. "On your birthday, you must welcome all your friends, old and new."

"Come in . . . Sandra . . ." said Mei Gwen reluctantly.

Sandra followed her down the hall. Everybody looked at Sandra when she entered the room and told her how pretty she was.

"She's not . . . she's not . . ." began Mei Gwen. She tried to explain that Dina Costelli and not Sandra Sung was her girlfriend, but no one listened.

"We are glad to see you, Sandra," said Mother. "Sit down and have a piece of Mei Gwen's birthday cake."

Shy and silent, Sandra sat down.

Then Father lighted the candles on the cake, brought it in, and Mei Gwen blew them out with one whiff. She hung her head shyly as they sang *Happy Birthday* in true American style.

They all gathered round while Mei Gwen cut the cake.

"I am glad you and Mei Gwen are such good friends," said Father. "One girl who lives on the second floor and one who lives on the fourth floor—should they not be good friends?"

Mei Gwen looked at Father in surprise. He well knew that the laundryman's daughter never washed her face or her dresses, because Mei Gwen had told him so herself. He well knew that she had never even spoken to this girl before. Why should he now call them *good friends?*

But Mei Gwen soon forgot Sandra in the birthday excitement, for she had all her birthday presents to open. She untied the pretty ribbons and took the pretty papers off the boxes. Aunty Kate and Uncle Fred gave her a new coat for winter. Aunty Rose and Uncle

Leon brought her a new skirt and blouse. There were a new dress from Mr. and Mrs. Yick and the twins, a pretty nightgown from Grandmother Yee, and a Chinese fan with blue roses on it from Cousins Dorinda and Jean. There was a beautiful pair of ivory chopsticks from Old Mr. Wong. The last two boxes contained new sweaters, one blue and one pink, exactly alike.

"How can I wear two sweaters?" asked Mei Gwen, laughing. "Is it going to be a very cold winter?"

She glanced at Sandra, who sat looking down in her lap with a sad expression on her face. Mei Gwen looked from Mother to Father. They seemed to be expecting something of her. All at once, she knew what to do.

"I will keep the blue one," she said. She took the pink sweater and laid it on Sandra Sung's lap. "You can play like it's your birthday today, too, Sandra," she said. "Here is your birthday present. It matches your dress exactly."

Sandra jumped up, put her arms around Mei Gwen and gave her a kiss. Mother smiled and Father beamed approval. All the others clapped.

Then Mother said she had a big surprise. She gave Mei Gwen three guesses. The girl guessed candy, fruit and flowers, but it was none of these. It was a pair of new roller skates. How happy Mei Gwen was when she saw them!

"Just what I've been wanting," she cried. "Now I can skate to the jeans factory every day as fast as lightning!"

"But not on Grant Avenue," said Mother. "There are too many cars and too many people there."

"Can you skate, Sandra?" asked Mei Gwen.

"Yes, I have some old skates," she said.

Father's surprise was last.

"Now that you are ten years old," Father said solemnly, "it is time for you to start to Chinese evening school. Most boys and girls start at a younger age, for there is much to learn. But we have waited until you have become accustomed to city life. You must learn to read and write Chinese as well as English. A Chinese in America must know both Chinese and English—even a woman, for women need learning, too, in this day and age. It is time for you to begin."

Father handed Mei Gwen a school bag and she slipped the strap over her shoulder. He showed her all the things inside it, the Chinese writing and reading books, ink box and brush.

"Is it hard work?" asked Mei Gwen.

"To do anything well is always hard work," said Father. "I will help you at home until you catch up with the others in your grade."

Now, last of all, Felix handed Mei Gwen a small box. She opened it and jumped back, asking, "Is it alive?"

"No," said Felix. "It is a pretty pin to wear on your coat." He pinned a silver turtle on her shoulder. "It won't bite you," he said. "It didn't come from the Yet Sang Fish Shop!"

Mei Gwen called the little children to play *Pin the Tail on the Donkey*. "Come, Sandra," she cried, "you can be first. Let me blindfold you." Soon the apartment was ringing with merriment. Old Mr. Wong played his butterfly harp and everybody was happy.

At last the party was over and the people went home. Sandra said good night and wished Mei Gwen good health and a long life like the others. She wore her new pink sweater and went down the stairs.

"I like your new girl-friend," said Mother. "She looked so pretty in her party dress. She is gentle and quiet and has nice manners."

Mei Gwen thought of Dina Costelli who had never come at all. Suddenly all her bitterness against Sandra came back.

"Sandra Sung is *not* my girl-friend at all!" she burst out impatiently. "I never even spoke to her before, let alone asking her to my party. She's always dirty and her clothes are torn and ragged. Why did she come in a party dress when it wasn't her birthday at all?"

"*I* asked her to come because she was lonely and unhappy," said Mother. "She had no nice dress to wear and I did not want her to feel embarrassed. So when I bought your party dress, I bought one for her. Her parents are poor and her mother has been sick. Sandra worked at the laundry when we first came, counting and folding towels and wrapping bundles. But now she stays at home, trying to take care of her sick mother and the younger children. Father has decided we shall send our clothes to their laundry to help them out. Could you not share a little of your happiness or are you entirely selfish?"

Mei Gwen hid her face, ashamed of herself.

"Oh, Mother," she cried. "I didn't know all that . . ."

"But now she is your girl-friend," said Mother.

"I'm glad I gave her the pink sweater," said Mei Gwen.

"A birthday marks the beginning of a new year," said Mother. "It is a day for growing up."

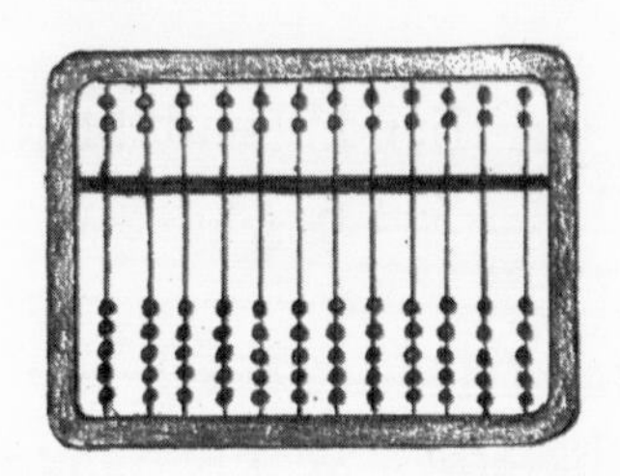

CHAPTER VII

A Walk in the Park

Mei Gwen came down the stairs carrying her new roller skates. Would Sandra be at home or working in the laundry? She knocked at the door of apartment No. 3, and Sandra opened it.

"Bring your skates and come to the jeans factory with me," said Mei Gwen. "We'll take the children to Portsmouth Square. Next week I have to go to Chinese school and I won't be baby sitter any more."

"Are you glad?" asked Sandra.

"I like being baby sitter," said Mei Gwen, "and I don't know if I'll like Chinese school or not."

Sandra brought her skates and the girls went downstairs. They sat on the outside doorstep. It was strange how quickly Sandra had turned into a good friend.

"My old skates got too small for me," said Mei Gwen, buckling on her new ones. "Frankie used them and lost them for me."

Across the street was the fire station. A large hose-and-ladder truck could be seen inside the open door. Mei Gwen waited while Sandra put on her skates.

"We've got everything in our block," said Mei Gwen. "A fire station, a restaurant, a beauty shop, a laundry and a grocery. Whenever we want anything, we can run out and get it. We are always safe in our apartment and I'll tell you why."

"Why?" asked Sandra.

"Right there is the fire station," said Mei Gwen, pointing. "If we holler and say, 'Our house is on fire,' Fireman George doesn't have to use his truck at all. He just walks across the street and puts the fire out. I know all the firemen, George and Donald and Fred. They speak English like American people. I say, 'Hi, fireman!' when I go past."

"I don't like to hear the siren," said Sandra. "It scares me and wakes me up at night."

"Just hold your hands tight over your ears and you won't hear it," said Mei Gwen. The girls got up and started skating. Mei Gwen pointed down the street.

"If I want to buy something for dinner, I can go in that restaurant," she said. "They cook Won Ton Pay—that's dough with meat wrapped up inside it—and I can take it home with me. If I want to buy eggs or rice or a Chinese brush, I go to the Fat Lung Grocery on the corner. If I want my dress washed and ironed, I go to the Sun Sun Laundry right over there."

Sandra laughed. She was proud of her father's laundry.

"If I want to get a permanent," Mei Gwen went on, "I *don't* go to the Jade Beauty Parlor. I go to my Aunty Kate's on Columbus Avenue and get it *for free*. But my father won't let me have one. He likes a straight bob for babies like Susie and he likes braids for me."

"Have you ever had a permanent?" asked Sandra.

"Oh no, it hurts," said Mei Gwen. "I don't like it—four hours of hurting your head! Oh no!"

"Still," said Sandra in a longing tone, thinking of her own long stringy hair, "it would be nice to have curls. . . ."

Mei Gwen held her nose tight. "That stuff they use smells bad," she said. "It's cold and it's heavy and they put your head in a big machine. I've watched my Aunty Kate do it. First it stings on one side, then it stings on the other. If you get it twice, your hair will turn brown and smell like a rotten fish."

At the corner of Washington Street, the girls waved their hands to Policeman Mike. Then they skated down the hill slowly. A noisy cable car passed by loaded with people. It kept going *clickety, clickety, click.*

"I love to ride on the cable car, don't you?" said Mei Gwen. She had not had many rides, but she liked to brag a little.

"My mother doesn't let me," said Sandra.

"Are you afraid?" asked Mei Gwen. "I like to ride on the outside seats and Elder Brother stands on the running board and holds on tight."

"I'm afraid," said Sandra. "I'd rather walk."

"There is nothing to be afraid of!" Mei Gwen tossed her head and spoke as if she were an experienced traveler. "On the cable car you can see out better than on the bus. On the cable car you go sight-seeing *for free,* no extra pay, only the regular fare. Once my mother took me on the bus through the tunnel and we went shopping on Market Street, where all the Americans go. But the bus was crowded and the people mashed me and stepped on my toes. I did not like it. The bus went faster, but I could not see out at all."

Mei Gwen wished Sandra could skate better, but she was having trouble with her skates. Suddenly one skate broke and she fell down. Two wheels came off and went rolling out into the street, just as another cable car came clanging along. They rolled right in front of the car.

The two girls stared in dismay. Would the cable car run over the wheels and break them? Or would the wheels land on the

track and wreck the cable car? Sandra started to run out into the street, and when Mei Gwen pulled her back, she began to cry. The conductor saw them and pulled the cord.

The cable car slowed up to allow an automobile to pass. The grip man pulled hard on his long brake handle. The car stopped and the conductor got out. Mei Gwen called out to him, "The wheels came off this girl's roller skates. They went under the cable car!"

The conductor reached under the car, picked up the wheels and brought them over to the curb. He brought them over to Sandra.

"A good thing they were too big to go down in the slot," he said. "That would have clogged up the cable." He climbed back on and waved his hand.

All the passengers were watching and smiling. The grip man pulled the long handle that gripped the cable in the slot below, and the cable car moved on. The girls waved until it turned into Powell Street.

"Too bad your skate broke," said Mei Gwen. "I'll ask my father to fix it for you."

Sandra had stopped crying and was cheerful again. She skated on one skate and carried the broken one. At last the girls came to Commercial Street, and there at the door of the factory, the little children were waiting. Mother and Aunty Rose said the two girls could take them to the park.

"Watch out for the cars when you cross the street," said Mother. Aunty Rose added, "Cross when the cars are a block away—if there is no light."

Just then Jessie Chong came out of her house across the street. "Where are you taking them?" she called.

Mei Gwen did not answer.

"Can I go along and help you?" asked Jessie.

Mei Gwen tossed her head and ignored her. She turned to Sandra and the little ones. "Let's play *Marching!*" she cried. "Let's have a parade!"

She lined the children up in pairs. At the head of the line, Mei Gwen pushed Susie in her stroller. Cousin Dorinda came next holding Cousin Jean's hand. Paul walked with James Gee, Larry Chew with his little brother Tom, and Sandra came last with little Lily Gee. There were only two corners to turn to get to Portsmouth Square, and a friendly policeman helped them across Kearny Street. The boys and girls made noises like a band play-

ing and drums beating as they stamped their feet.

Once in the park, the procession broke up. All the children ran for the swings and slides. Mei Gwen and Sandra had a busy time pushing them and helping them up and down. The crowd was not large, the grass was green and the trees were shady. The park was a pleasant change from the sidewalks and from the dark, dusty interior of the factory.

Cousin Paul and James Gee, who were five, loved to dig in the sand pile. Mei Gwen was helping them build hills and roads for their toy cars, when someone called her. Looking up, she saw Felix, and with him, Frankie and Freddie. Felix was carrying the butterfly kite that Uncle Fred had made for him.

"What are you doing here?" asked Mei Gwen.

"I stopped for the boys after school," said Felix, "the way you told me to. But they were not there. A boy in their class told me they were with Harry Lum and that Harry was going to fly his eagle kite. So I went home and got mine. There's a good wind today."

Harry Lum, a boy of fourteen, came down the walk carrying a large eagle kite made of transparent purple paper mounted on fine sticks of bamboo. Frankie and Freddie and other children crowded close to see it. Soon Sammy Hong appeared with his fish kite. Felix brought his butterfly kite and joined them. They walked to the lower part of the park, away from the trees.

"Aw, this is no place to fly kites," said Sammy Hong. "I always go out to the Marina. There's a good wind from the ocean out there at Aquatic Park."

"Yes, but it's too far," said Harry. "We haven't time to go so far today. Let's have our contest now and see who is the winner. Let's see who can stay up the longest."

Mei Gwen and Sandra lined the little children up again and they all watched. People in the park crowded up to see. The three boys ran with their kites against the wind, loosening the strings, and soon the fish, the eagle and the butterfly were soaring as high as the buildings around the square. Now the contest really began, as each boy tried to fight the other kites, manipulating his string to cut or break the strings of his opponents.

Felix ran breathlessly, pulling hard to keep his kite up. Would the eagle or the fish win? They were both larger and stronger than his butterfly. But the butterfly, though small, was wiry and tough. It stayed up, carried along steadily by the wind, while the eagle and the fish fell face downward and had to be raised aloft again.

It was very exciting to watch. Frankie and Freddie kept running after the kite flyers and Felix had to shout to them to stay back. Time slipped by, and Chinese school was completely forgotten.

Suddenly Mei Gwen heard her name called. There was Aunty Rose at the street corner, making motions for her to come and bring the children back to the factory.

"Sandra, let's take the children marching again," said Mei Gwen.

Off across the busy street the little procession went. The children watched the kites as long as they could see them. By the time Mei Gwen and Sandra returned to the park, the kite contest was over.

"Sammy's fish won," said Felix at the corner. "Everybody said it was unfair. Sammy Hong had razor blades on his string. His string crossed Harry's and cut it—so the eagle went flying. Harry was mad about it—he hated to lose a wonderful kite like that. He started to beat Sammy up, but Sammy's father was sitting there on a bench all the time watching. He put a quick stop to the fight."

"How did you come out?" asked Mei Gwen.

"My pretty little butterfly didn't stand a chance," said Felix. "And poor Harry went home disgusted. At least I've still got my kite, and of course, Sammy still has his." He looked around. "Now where have Frankie and Freddie gone? You go on home—I'll have to hunt for them."

Mei Gwen and Sandra sat on a bench and put on their roller skates. They went skating off up Clay Street, Mei Gwen on two skates, Sandra on one. When they reached home, they put their skates in Sandra's apartment. Sandra brought out a ball and they played ball until Sandra fell and hurt her knee. Then her mother called her from their front bay window, so she went in. Mei Gwen went up to the top floor. She pulled out her chain and started to unlock the door. But her key was gone.

She looked again. Her identification tag and her skate key were there, but the door key was gone. Had she dropped it when she opened the chain to put the skate key on? She hunted in the hallway, but it wasn't there. She went down to Sandra's door and asked her about it, but Sandra knew nothing.

"How can I get in?" cried Mei Gwen, nearly in tears. "I'm locked out. What will I do? My mother will punish me when she finds I've lost my door key."

"Why don't you ask Felix what to do?" suggested Sandra.

"I don't even know where Felix is," said Mei Gwen. "He's hunting for Frankie and Freddie, and won't get home until late at night."

"Your mother will let you in," said Sandra.

"And punish me," added Mei Gwen. "She's working late tonight, too."

"Come in here and wait until she comes," said Sandra. But Mei Gwen started sadly down the stairs. "Where are you going?"

"Back to Portsmouth Square," said Mei Gwen. "I've got to find that key before Mother gets home. I think I dropped it by that bench where we put our skates on to come home."

Mei Gwen looked in the grass and on the sidewalk at the park, but she could not find her door key. She watched a group of girls playing on the grass, but they did not ask her to join them. She listened as they chanted their counting-out rhyme:

"My mother and your mother live across the street,
Sixteen, seventeen, eight Broadway;
Every time they have a fight
This is what they say:
Eecka, acka, bluebird,
Eecka, acka, out!"

Mei Gwen looked again for the key, then decided to go home. She walked up Washington Street, and was passing the public school when she heard the siren of an ambulance. Holding her hands over her ears, she saw the ambulance go whizzing up the hill. She heard a commotion and saw people running. Up at the corner of Washington and Mason something had happened. She ran too. A crowd had gathered.

"A little girl is hurt," a man said. "She tried to cross on a red light, and an automobile struck her."

The ambulance whizzed away with its little victim, leaving Policeman Mike talking to the car owner and questioning bystanders. Soon all the excitement was over.

Mei Gwen remembered that Mother had told her to bring something from the store. What was it? She could not think. She walked into the Fat Lung Grocery on the corner. She looked for her friend, Uncle Kee, but he was not there. The store was empty. Where had Uncle Kee gone?

Beside the door was a gum machine. Mei Gwen looked in the purse that was chained to her belt. She took out a penny and put it in the slot. She got a stick of gum and chewed it. She put in another penny and got another stick. What she wanted was a

charm, and her third penny brought her one—a tiny rocket ship. She put it carefully inside her purse. It would be nice to hang on her good-luck bracelet. She wanted a watch or a heart or a four-leaf clover, but alas, her pennies were all gone.

Mei Gwen went into the store again and looked around. She picked up a jar of hard American candies and looked at their pretty colors. Suddenly something moved. She jumped and dropped the jar, frightened. It fell on the counter but did not break. There stood Uncle Kee beside her. A curtain had been pulled aside and there he was.

"What! A customer!" said Mr. Kee. "Neighbor Fong's

daughter! What does your mother need today, young lady?"

Mei Gwen stopped trembling. He took no notice of the dropped candy jar. "My mother told me to bring something, but I forget what she wanted."

"Some *dow gawk* (long Chinese beans)? Some *foo qwa* (bitter melon)? Some lotus root or soybean cakes? Some *dung chee* (Chinese rice tamale)?"

The more things Uncle Kee suggested, the more confused Mei Gwen became.

Uncle Kee vanished behind the curtain again. Soon he came out with two smoked spareribs on a small plate, and offered them to Mei Gwen. She took the paper napkin in her hand, picked them up and ate them. She put the bones back on the plate and licked her lips.

"Good?" asked Uncle Kee. "They taste good?"

"Yes, thank you, Uncle Kee," said Mei Gwen.

"You had better go home now," said Mr. Kee gently, "or your mother will think you are lost."

Tears came to Mei Gwen's eyes. "It is not I but my key that is lost," she said. "I am afraid to go home without it. I can't get in."

"Why not telephone your mother?" suggested Mr. Kee.

Mei Gwen looked in her purse, but it was empty. She had spent her last three pennies, and she had no nickels or dimes. "I have no money," she said. "I have spent it all."

"Here is a dime," said Mr. Kee.

Mei Gwen put the dime in the slot and dialed the number, but there was no answer. The dime was returned and she gave it back to Mr. Kee.

"Nobody is at home," said Mei Gwen sadly. "My mother is working late tonight. There is a rush order on."

"Call her at the factory," said Mr. Kee.

"Oh no," said Mei Gwen. "She scolds me if I do that. It interrupts her work. She can't stop to answer the phone."

"Wait a little longer then," said Mr. Kee cheerfully. "Your mother will soon come home."

Customers came into the store and he was kept busy. Mei Gwen waited patiently by the open door. Suddenly a woman came rushing up on the sidewalk.

"Where is she? Where is my little girl?" she cried. "Where did the ambulance go? What hospital did they take her to? Did a car bump into her?"

People on the street crowded round the woman, trying to answer her, all talking at once. Suddenly Mei Gwen realized it was her own mother.

"Oh, Mother!" cried Mei Gwen, rushing out. "I'm not hurt. I was waiting in here with Uncle Kee. That was some strange girl who was taken to the hospital. It wasn't me!"

Mother Fong took Mei Gwen in her arms and held her tight.

"When I got home so late and found you were not there, I came out on the street looking and they told me an automobile had struck somebody—"

"I lost my door key, Mother, and I couldn't get in," said Mei Gwen. "I forgot which vegetable you wanted me to buy . . . and Felix is out hunting for Frankie and Freddie. . . ."

But Mother was not thinking of keys or runaway boys or Chinese vegetables. "Thank God you are safe," she said.

CHAPTER VIII

A Day to Go Fishing

"Oh, I want to ride on the cable car!" cried Mei Gwen.

Father smiled. "You do not wish to walk?"

"It's real far to Fisherman's Wharf, eighteen blocks," said Mei Gwen. "I walk up the hill, down the hill, up the hill, down, then flat, and at last I get there. I walked it once and I know!"

Father laughed.

"I can walk there in half an hour," said Felix, "or run in fifteen minutes."

"You will have enough walking to do after you get there," said Father, "so you'd better take the cable car." He passed out money for carfare, fifteen cents for each and ten cents each for ice cream.

"But I'm afraid to ride on the outside seat," said Mei Gwen. "I'd be scared to go round the corner."

"If you sit inside and hold on tight," said Father, "you will not be in danger."

"Here is your lunch," said Mother.

She gave the children a paper bag containing tuna-fish sandwiches and apples. Sometimes on Saturdays, the Fongs planned holiday trips for their children to various parts of the city. Today they were going to meet Mei Gwen's Italian friend, Dina Costelli, at Fisherman's Wharf. Mei Gwen had seen the girl again at her father's store and arranged it.

"Maybe we'll see somebody fishing," said Felix. "I used to fish with a red string in Alameda and it always brought me luck. When I grow up and make some money, I'm going to buy a place in Alameda. Then I can go fishing every day."

"Take care of Frankie and Freddie," said Mother. "Don't let them get lost, or fall in San Francisco Bay."

Father's final advice to the children was serious.

"My children, you were born in America and have lived here all your lives," he said. "Therefore you are Americans. Although you are of the Chinese race, you feel like Americans. But remember, the tourists who come to San Francisco from all parts of the country think of you as Chinese. Many of them have never seen Chinese children before. So you must always be thoughtful, polite and courteous, for you are representing your race. Do not do anything to make me ashamed of you."

The sun was shining brightly as they started out. The children climbed on the first cable car that came. Mei Gwen sat down on an inside seat and soon forgot to be scared. Frankie and Freddie sat on the open seat that faced outward. Felix stood on the running board and held to the bar handle. He wore no hat, so his hair was soon blowing in the breeze.

Up and down over the hills, along Mason Street and into Columbus Avenue, the cable car rattled and bumped along. At the end of the line, it came to the turntable, where all the passengers got off. The children watched as the grip man and conductor pushed the tiny car around to face the other way. When it started back to town again, they walked several blocks and came to Fisherman's Wharf.

Down at the water front the smell of the sea was strong. White-winged gulls circled overhead screeching. The wharf was a busy place. Along the covered sidewalk crowds of tourists were strolling, looking in at shop windows and buying souvenirs. On the curb were counters where seafood was sold, and tanks filled with boiling water where live crabs were cooked to order. The children walked slowly, trying to see everything.

Mei Gwen held her nose. "I don't like this fishy smell," she said.

"Here's where all the fish come from," said Felix, "so you've got to smell them. How do you know that Italian girl is going to meet you? She never came to your birthday party like she said she would."

"She said she's not allowed to go out at night," said Mei Gwen. "That's why she couldn't come to my party. But she and her two brothers come to Fisherman's Wharf every Saturday. She's going to meet me by Romano's Restaurant at ten o'clock. She knows all the best places to go."

"But I thought we were going fishing," said Frankie. "I want to get in a boat and catch a fish."

"We have no boat or hooks or poles or lines," said Felix. "How can we go fishing?"

"Let's go where the fishermen are," said Freddie. "I want to watch them. I want to see them pull a big whale out of the water."

The children read the signs on all the fish restaurants. At last they came to Romano's, and there was Dina Costelli standing beside the door. It was ten minutes after ten by the big clock inside.

"I thought you were never coming," said Dina. "I've been waiting over an hour. We got here early."

"The cable car was so slow," said Mei Gwen. "We almost had to get out and push!"

Dina turned to the little boys. "Do you want to see two sea

lions? Live ones?" she asked. "Come, I will take you there."

Down the street, the barking of sea lions could be plainly heard. A short walk brought the children to a huge water tank on the sidewalk. It was enclosed in glass and the boys pushed up close to see. One sea lion was resting on a platform at the end, the other was snorting in the water. Tourists crowded around on all sides. Some paid fifteen cents for a small envelope of dry sardines and fed them. The sea lions jumped to catch the sardines, often turning somersaults. The water splashed out through an opening at the top and gave the boys a shower bath. They jumped back, laughing.

All this time, Mei Gwen kept her distance.

"Are you afraid?" asked Dina. "Those lazy old sea lions can't hurt you."

But Mei Gwen had seen enough. "Now where do we go?" she asked.

"You want to see my father's boat?" asked Dina. "If he is there, we can go on it."

"Whoopee!" cried Freddie. "We will go on the boat and catch a big fish! We will fry it and eat it all up."

"But the boat is in the harbor now," said Dina. "My father has to go across the bay and under Golden Gate Bridge and out into the Pacific Ocean to catch his fish. The men stay two or three days and come back with a big load, sometimes twenty thousand pounds. The dragnet goes down to the bottom of the ocean and brings up all kinds of fish—rock cod, codfish, flounder, sand dabs and sole."

"But I thought people could catch fish right here at Fisherman's

Wharf," said Frankie, "with a pole and line."

"We used to fish on the other side of the bay when we lived in Alameda," said Felix. "We fished with poles and lines."

"Oh sure," said Dina. "Some kids do that here, too. My brothers, they spend all their free time fishing. They're here today somewhere. They brought all their fishing gear along. They've got a bunch of junk to fish with. . . ."

"Where are they?" asked Felix, getting excited.

"I don't know," said Dina. "It would be hard to find them."

They walked along the street, then turned in at one of the piers. Here the square lagoon was lined on three sides with colorful fishing boats. There were small, bright-colored crab-fishing boats and larger, tall-masted sardine trawlers. Expensive Italian restaurants with large windows overlooked the lagoon. They

stopped to watch a man lift steaming crabs from a tank of boiling water. Then Dina led the children around to the place where her father's boat was tied up.

"There it is—the *Angelina,*" she said. "It's a bottom-fish trawler."

The tide was out and all the boats lay so low in the water, it was not possible to board the *Angelina.* Not far away a long brown net was spread out on the wharf to dry. An old man, wearing a stocking cap, knelt at one end with a shuttle and cord in his hand. He was mending holes in the net.

Dina spoke to him in Italian and he answered with a smile. But the Chinese children did not understand what he said.

"What's that funny language he's talking?" asked Frankie.

"Italian," said Dina.

"It sounds funny to us," said Mei Gwen, "just like Chinese sounds funny to you."

"Old Tony says all the boats are in today because of rough weather," explained Dina. "He thinks it's going to storm before tonight. He says it takes five or six hours to get out to the place where they fish. They start about midnight, so they can fish in the daytime. They come back about eight at night and unload all their fish."

"Does he know where your brothers are?" asked Felix.

Dina spoke to Old Tony. He answered, pointing to a pier farther away.

"Tony says they are at the Hyde Street pier," said Dina. "I will take you boys there, and then Mei Gwen will come with me to my house. My mother wants to see her."

Dina and Mei Gwen took the boys to Hyde Street and left them there. The pier was deserted except for one parked car. No tourists were strolling there and no souvenirs were for sale. A group of young boys were busily fishing. Dina pointed out her brothers Georgie and Joey. With them were three Mexican boys and a small colored boy. Felix and his two little brothers came up to watch.

Georgie and Joey were bell-fishing. A stiff strong wire was attached by a clothes hook to the plank at the edge of the pier. It stood up in the air and at the top there was a jingle bell. Down from the bell a fishing line dangled into the water below. When the fish began to bite the bait on the hook, the bell jingled.

Hearing the bell ring, Joey called out, "Come and spear them! Come and spear them, Georgie! It looks like striped bass!"

Georgie took his spear—a frog spear which he had bought at a fish-supply store—and hurried down a ladder to try his luck. The other boys lay down on the pier and looked over the edge. Georgie had scraped barnacles and small mussels off the piling with his knife and had crushed them up. Now he threw several handfuls into the water to attract the fish.

"Striped bass swim on top of the water," said Georgie. "If you use barnacles and mussels for bait, they come up quick."

Georgie had a cloth sack tied to his belt to put the fish in when he caught them. But no fish appeared. He was too late. The bass had swum past.

"Aw, shucks!" said the Negro boy. "That guy don't know how to fish. He hasn't caught anything all morning. I'm tired of watching him."

"He thinks he knows all about fishing," said the oldest Mexican boy, "but he can't catch a thing. Come on, guys, let's go."

The four boys left the pier, disgusted. Now Felix was alone with his two brothers and the two Italian boys.

"Maybe the water's too rough today," said Felix. "That old fisherman, Tony, said it's going to storm before night."

"The best time to get fish," said Georgie, "is when the tide is rough, going in or going out, very rough like today. The most we ever caught was on a day just like this—fourteen pile perch in one day."

"How big were they?" asked Felix.

"The small ones were twelve inches," said Georgie, "the big ones, twenty inches. I used the spear for the biggest, and Joey used the hook for the small ones."

Felix thought of the red string and can of worms he had used in Alameda. How young and silly he was then! That kind of fishing was a joke! Felix forgot that the Costelli boys were strangers. He talked to them as if he had known them all his life. They showed him all their fishing tackle. They had many things he had never seen before—all kinds of weights and hooks and nets and poles and lines and spears. They explained all the clever tricks they had invented. The Italian boys, on the other hand, recognized a true fisherman when they saw one.

"I will tell you a secret," said Georgie in a low whisper. "I tell this to only a few of my best friends. *We go under the pier to fish.* That is the best place. That is our secret. You will not tell other people?"

"No," said Felix. "I will keep your secret. I will not even tell my little brothers. They have not sense enough to keep a secret."

"You want me to show you the place under the pier where we go?" asked Georgie.

"Yes," said Felix. "But first I will give my little brothers their lunch and tell them to go for a walk. I will give each of them ten cents to spend for ice cream. While they are gone, you can show me."

Felix gave Frankie and Freddie sandwiches and money, and they ran off happily. They were not interested in fishing and were glad to explore.

"Come back here in half an hour," said Felix sternly. Hastily he ate his own sandwich and apple. Georgie gave him an extra spear to use.

"Try and see if you can do it," said Georgie. "With a little practice, it will come easy."

Felix followed the Costelli boys still farther out on the pier. A chilly wind had come up and it began to be cold in spite of the bright sun. The whole bay was rough with whitecaps. The boys came to an opening in the dock where they climbed down a crude ladder. Below, double planks were laid across heavy beams, the substructure of the pier itself. It was high tide and the choppy waves came almost up to the planks.

Georgie and Joey showed no fear of the rough water so close beneath them. Felix was not afraid either, but he was cold without a jacket. How wonderful to be with boys who loved fishing and the water as he did! The three boys crouched on the planks, spears in hand, waiting for fish to come.

After a time Georgie became restless and started for a new

location. He walked the planks as if he were walking a tight rope.

"Are you ever afraid, Georgie," asked Felix.

"No," said Georgie. "I just balance myself and walk real fast!"

"Did you ever fall in?" asked Felix.

"No, but Joey did once," said Georgie. "We were getting rock cods at low tide under the pier. They came out from under the rocks and Joey grabbed them and put them in a sack. Then all at once he slipped on a wet rock and went in water up to his waist. He had to sit on the pier to get his clothes dry. Lucky it was a hot day in summer."

Felix and Joey laughed. Then Joey pointed and cried, "Look!"

All three boys stared. There, about ten feet away, they saw a sea lion rising on top of the water. It came up for about five seconds, then dove back down. Georgie came closer holding his

spear firmly with his two hands, hoping to spear it. The sea lion rose once or twice more, then it was gone.

"That's better than those tame ones out in the tank on the street," said Felix.

"Gee, I wish I could spear a sea lion once," said Georgie. "I've only caught one perch today. For perch, summer is best. Sometimes we catch many, and sometimes none at all."

Felix smiled. "Fisherman's luck!" he said. Suddenly he remembered his younger brothers and his responsibility. "Is it half an hour?" he asked, glancing at Joey's wrist watch. "Have my brothers been gone half an hour?"

"More than that," said Joey. "It's a quarter after two already."

"Aw—let them take care of themselves," said Georgie. "Stay and fish with us. I will teach you everything I know—"

"No, I must go," said Felix. "My younger brothers haven't much sense and they might get into trouble. I have to keep an eye on them." He hesitated, hating to leave, then he asked, "Could I come and fish with you some other time, Georgie?"

"Sure, sure," said Georgie, grinning, "any time you want. You be my partner, we catch lots of fish and sell it to people I know—to houses and to stores. Maybe you sell yours in Chinatown, eh?"

"I know Mr. Ben Lum," said Felix, "in the Yet Sang Fish Shop on Grant Avenue."

"Good, good!" said Georgie. "You come back again, any time. We come fishing every Saturday, and Sunday after church, and holidays. We come early about seven o'clock and we stay till three or four o'clock, and go home when we get tired. Get yourself a pole and line and hooks and some little sandbags, and

I will let you use my bells and nets and all kinds of things."

Felix hated to go but he had to. When he climbed up the ladder, he saw no one. Even the parked car was gone. Where were the boys? And wasn't it time for Mei Gwen to be back? Where did that girl take her?

"The boys have run away again," said Felix to himself.

He started out on what seemed like a hopeless search. He went back to the lagoon where the *Angelina* was tied up. He watched men working on two fishing boats in drydock. They were scraping and painting the bottoms of the boats. He saw Old Tony still mending his nets.

"Where are my brothers?" he asked. "Have you seen them?"

Tony understood. He pointed to a group of boys at the far end of the wharf, in front of a large restaurant. Felix went over. The boys were crowding around a little fellow who held something in his hand. Felix bent over and saw a tiny dried sea horse. The American boys were very excited. They had probably never seen one before.

"Aw, nuts!" said the little fellow on the ground. "We *eat* them. We eat them alive and we eat their dried bony skeletons too! Sea horses keep us healthy. You ought to come to Chinatown and see."

Felix listened in astonishment, for the voice sounded familiar. He looked more closely—it was Frankie. What wild tales was Frankie telling? Felix thought of Father. Was this the best way for a small Chinese boy to represent his race?

"Frankie!" cried Felix, sternly. "Get up and come here."

Frankie got up and hung his head.

"Tell the boys that's not true—all you've been saying," said Felix.

"But the herb doctor *does* use dried sea horses for medicine, said Frankie. "I heard Grandmother say so. And we *do* eat lots of things that Americans don't eat—pressed ducks and frogs and eels and snails . . ."

"Frankie! Come with me," said Felix.

Frankie handed the dried sea horse to a boy standing near. "Here, take it," he said. "You can eat it to make you healthy!"

The American boys laughed and went on their way. Frankie followed his older brother sheepishly.

"Where's Freddie?" asked Felix.

"I don't know," said Frankie. "He ran away and left me."

They were passing Romano's Restaurant, one of the famous

eating places in San Francisco. The large plate-glass windows faced the busy harbor where the fishing boats lay at anchor. Inside, the tables were covered with white tablecloths and many people were eating. Felix and Frankie looked inside.

"Look!" cried Frankie suddenly. "There's Freddie."

"Where?" asked Felix.

"In there, sitting at that table, eating!" cried Frankie.

Felix could not believe his eyes. There, inside, sat Freddie at a table with two gentlemen and two ladies, people he had never seen before, strangers—Americans. They were all talking and laughing gaily. Freddie, with his mouth full, was trying to talk, too. Freddie was using knife, fork and spoon as if he had never seen chopsticks in all his life.

Suddenly Freddie saw his two brothers outside the window. His eyes fell. He dropped his fork, spoke to his new friends and quickly left the table. The next minute he was on the sidewalk beside his brothers.

Felix looked at him severely. "Younger Brother, *how did you get in there?*" he asked.

"I . . . I . . . I was hungry," explained Freddie. "After I ate my sandwich, I was still hungry. Those crabs the men were cooking on the sidewalk made me more hungry. To see those people eating in the restaurant and to smell all that good food made me still *more* hungry . . ."

"But how did you get *in*?" asked Felix.

"I put my face close up to the window," said Freddie. "I wanted to see what that man was eating. It was a great big boiled crab! The man saw me and he came out and gave me a crab leg to eat. That made me still MORE hungry. He offered me money, but I would not take it. I told him I do not take money from strangers. So he said, 'Come in and I'll buy you a good meal for once in your life,' and I went. That's how I got in."

"He thought you were starving, I suppose," said Felix. "Did you tell him you get plenty to eat at home and that your father is head-cook at the Lotus Garden Restaurant in Chinatown and that you can get all you want to eat there any time you want it?"

"No, I didn't," said Freddie. "I never thought of that."

"Some day I hope you will get some sense," said Felix. "Go in and thank the gentleman. Tell him you must now go home with your elder brother."

Felix and Frankie watched Freddie shake hands with the two gentlemen and two ladies at the table. They watched him make a polite bow and say goodbye. When he came outside again, Felix said briefly, "It is time to go home."

Felix knew it would be hard to explain this to Father and Mother. He had heard Father say that a generation before, when they were young, Chinese children had little opportunity or none to make friends outside their own race. Mother remembered the first time she ever saw a Caucasian face and how it frightened her —the protruding nose, the blue eyes so deeply set, the skin so pale and white. Mother could not get used to the fact that her children made friends of Americans and strangers so easily. What would she say when she heard that Freddie had *eaten* with them in a big expensive restaurant?

The boys walked solemnly along the street, thinking. They had not gone far, when Mei Gwen came running up behind them.

"Oh, I was almost lost!" she cried. "I could not find you anywhere. I looked on the Hyde Street pier and all the other piers for you. Dina hunted too—until she had to go home. What did you do? Where have you been?"

"We had a good time," said Felix with a smile. That seemed to cover everything. "What did *you* do?"

"Dina took me home with her," said Mei Gwen, bursting with enthusiasm, "and we ate spaghetti with Italian gravy. Her mother makes *fogaccia,* a sweet cake with raisins in it. And there's another kind, *torta,* and it's got spinach and lots of funny things in it, but it's good . . ."

What! More eating with strangers—Italians this time, thought Felix, smiling. How could he explain all this?

"Dina likes to sing," Mei Gwen went on, "and her father wants her to be a great singer and sing in Italian opera. Her grandmother sits and cries about the olive groves in Italy. She's as bad as Grandmother Yee—she came from Italy forty years ago and she's still homesick. Why do old people cry to go back to the place where they were born?"

All the way back to Chinatown in the cable car, Mei Gwen talked about her new-found friends. But Felix treasured the thought of Georgie and Joey inside his heart, and said nothing.

CHAPTER IX

A Day of Trouble

"I know where there's a haunted house," said Roger. "It's spooky."

"Where?" asked Felix.

"Up on Clay Street, on that little mountain there," said Roger. "On that empty lot behind the trees, way up high."

Roger and Felix were delivering papers on Stockton Street. Sammy Hong and Ronnie Chow had joined them.

"How do you know it's haunted?" asked Felix.

Sammy answered. "Some of the windows are broken," he said, "and the door is always blowing back and forth in the wind. Once I threw a ball in—Bang! It knocked something over inside and made another door slam. Something screeched and let out a terrible groan."

"Maybe the hinges needed oiling," said Ronnie.

"I bet Felix would be afraid to go inside," said Sammy. He looked at Roger and Ronnie and winked.

"Right back of it," said Roger, "there's a big high apartment building with zigzag steps that go up and up. Halfway up you come to the Drop Dead Place. . . ."

"Bet Felix would be afraid to jump off the Drop Dead Place," said Sammy.

"Let's show it to Felix," said Ronnie. "If he don't want to drop off, we could give him a shove." The boys laughed.

"Can't go now," said Roger in a businesslike tone. "We have to take these papers around."

"Let Felix finish the route," said Sammy.

"No, I'll go with him," said Roger. "We're partners. We'll meet you back at this corner in fifteen minutes."

Felix said nothing. He and Roger walked on down the street and into several buildings, leaving papers for customers. Felix trusted Roger but was uncertain about Sammy and Ronnie. For so long the boys had kept him feeling an outsider. Now he was determined to do whatever they said, even visit a haunted house. He knew Sammy was just trying to scare him. He would show Sammy he was no coward. A haunted house! What a joke!

In a short time Felix and Roger came back to the corner and met the other two boys. Ronnie had his soapbox scooter with him and Sammy had roller skates. Ronnie's scooter was a beauty. It had an aerial in front, a grinning face painted on the box, and roller-skate wheels underneath. Ronnie had made it himself.

"Let's coast downhill," said Felix.

"No," said Sammy. "We're going to the haunted house like we said."

It did not take long to get there. A high grassy lot rose steeply behind some large billboards. On the Clay Street side, a long flight of wooden steps led up to a rickety house. A pile of wood and trash could be seen at the top.

"Gee! They're tearing it down," said Roger.

"Let's go up and see," said Sammy.

Ronnie parked his scooter behind the billboard and the boys climbed the steps. Felix counted—there were fifty-six steps. At the top, they had to crawl over the fallen lumber.

"Listen!" said Sammy. "I don't hear any pounding. The workmen have gone away."

"They've left it to the spooks," said Ronnie grinning. "Somebody died here and the ghost is still hanging around."

Sammy picked up a stick and threw it in an open window. It fell with a dull thud and made a loud echo. Ronnie and Roger began to throw stones in.

"Felix, go in and chase the ghost out!" cried Sammy.

Ronnie threw another stone. This time, a real screech resounded through the building. Ronnie turned white.

"There's someone in there," he whispered. "It *is* haunted, after all. Gee, I'm scared!"

It took a lot to scare Sammy. He turned now to Felix. "Go in, Felix, and chase the ghost out. You wanted to see if the house was haunted. Now's your chance."

Felix looked about him uncertainly.

"I'll go in with you, Felix," said Roger.

"No, Roger," said Felix. "I want to go by myself."

The three other boys stood back and watched Felix enter the

open door. They waited, unsure of themselves and half-frightened. When they heard voices inside the house, they looked at each other in alarm. There *was* somebody in there, after all.

"We'd better scram!" said Sammy, running toward the top of the steps.

"Yes—scoot!" said Ronnie, running too.

"You go," said Roger. "I'll wait here for Felix."

Sammy and Ronnie scrambled over the fallen lumber and down the steps. Soon Roger saw Felix coming out of the door, unharmed. With him was a small, gray-haired woman, wearing a straw hat with a feather. She held a hurt cat in her arms. Quickly she made her way around the lumber to the top of the stairs. She shook her fist at the two boys hurrying down. She scolded them for throwing stones at cats.

"There are always cats in empty buildings," she said. "They are looking for food. I climbed up all those stairs just to feed them. I hate to see animals go hungry."

Felix and Roger had often seen the Cat Lady feeding cats in the dark alleys of Chinatown. They helped her down the long flight of steps. At the bottom she found her shopping cart, thanked the boys, and went on her way. As soon as she was out of sight, Sammy and Ronnie came back. They did not mention the haunted house.

"Let's coast down the hill," said Sammy, putting on his roller skates.

"Want to scoot down on my scooter, Felix?" asked Ronnie. He winked at Sammy. "You like steep hills, don't you?"

"I dare you to scoot all the way down to Grant Avenue without stopping once," said Sammy.

"O. K.," said Felix quietly. He had made up his mind he would do everything they wanted him to do.

The boys walked across the street on a green light. Felix took Ronnie's scooter and started on down ahead with it. Sammy came behind on his skates, and Ronnie and Roger followed yelling.

Felix went very fast, for the hill was steep. He zoomed along, going in and out among the people who were walking. Once he

nearly skidded into a water plug. He passed the entrance to several alleys, avoided hitting a child in a stroller, and zipped across Powell Street on a green light just ahead of a cable car. On through the next block, passing the open lot back of the public school to Stockton Street he went. The boys came behind, cheering him on. Felix felt very proud of himself.

The next block was not so easy, for there were more stores, with baskets and boxes of produce set out on the sidewalk. There were more people too, customers trying to make up their minds what to buy.

"Watch out! There's a cop!" called Roger behind.

Felix heard, looked quickly around, wondering if the boys were fooling, or if Policeman Mike would catch him. That one backward glance was his undoing. Zoom! Right into the outdoor wall-shop at the corner of Grant Avenue he went, knocking baskets and benches over and scattering toys and souvenirs all over the street.

Felix fell, hit his head on something hard and fainted. When he woke up, he was dazed and his knee pained him badly. He tried to get up. He could hardly stand on his feet because his legs hurt and he was dizzy. Roger helped him. "Lean on me," said Roger, kicking the scooter to one side.

The storekeeper, who had been sitting quietly reading his Chinese newspaper, jumped up and shouted, "Whose worthless son are you that you so disgrace your honorable father by wrecking a man's livelihood?"

Felix opened his eyes and saw that it was Mr. Chew, one of his best paper customers, the friendly storekeeper who often gave

him lichee nuts and Chinese candies. He saw, too, that Policeman Mike was hurrying over. A crowd of people had gathered and everybody had something to say. The whole neighborhood seemed to know what had happened.

Ronnie crept under a woman's elbow to rescue his scooter. But the woman saw him and held him.

"Here's the guilty boy," she said. "With his crazy soapbox scooter, he breaks up a man's business! All his livelihood ruined!"

"No, it was that other boy." A man pointed to Felix. "He was riding it, I saw him come down the hill, endangering the life of everybody on the street. Right on the sidewalk, too."

"But he is badly hurt," said another woman. "Look! Poor boy! He's hurt—he can't even stand up. Why doesn't somebody do something?"

Another woman spoke up. It was Mrs. Ping from Apartment No. 5 on the third floor of the Fongs' apartment house. "Why, he is the son of my neighbor, Frank Fong. He is cook at that fine restaurant, the Lotus Garden, on Grant Avenue. His children are well-behaved, an example to all the neighbors."

A businessman said, "He is the paper boy, who carries the *Call-Bulletin.*"

Mr. Chew spoke up quickly, "Is this boy Frank Fong's son?"

Policeman Mike did not smile and act friendly as usual. He asked the boys their names and wrote them down in a notebook. Then he turned briskly to Mr. Chew. "You want me to arrest him?" he asked. "The boy on the scooter who smashed up your shop? You want to bring charges?"

"Perhaps his father . . ." began Mr. Chew.

Ronnie squeezed into the crowd again to rescue his scooter.

"*There's* the boy!" said the woman. "It's *his* scooter. Arrest *him*!"

But Ronnie was too quick. He dodged back again and made off with his scooter. Sammy disappeared too.

"You want me to arrest him?" asked the policeman impatiently, holding Felix by the arm. "You want to bring suit for damages?"

Mr. Chew had had time to think, and now he spoke solemnly in Chinese, while all the bystanders listened. "I am a wise and thoughtful man," he said. "I have but one wish and that is to live in peace with my neighbors. We Chinese do not like to take our Chinese boys to court. We believe it is the father's duty to reprimand the son when he behaves badly. I will go to the boy's father, who is a responsible man. He will pay for the damage the boy has unintentionally done. The boy is young and has not yet learned the ways of wisdom. I could not face the boy's father if I had his son thrown into jail."

"Well, what's he saying anyhow?" Policeman Mike looked at Mrs. Ping. "Does he want me to arrest the kid?"

"No," said Mrs. Ping. "He will settle it with the boy's father."

Policeman Mike shrugged his shoulders. "O. K.," he said.

Suddenly Felix looked up and there he saw Younger Sister in the crowd. Mei Gwen was looking at him, shocked and surprised. Felix hung his head in shame. She had heard all this talk about being arrested and thrown into jail. The next minute she was gone. Would she tell Father everything? Had she gone to Chinese school or home to report? The policeman left, the crowd thinned out and Felix and Roger were left standing there.

Mr. Chew lifted his hands in despair as he looked at his shop. Straw hats and baskets, tops and airplanes, postcards, fruit, cigarettes, boxes of tea, Chinese slippers and souvenirs were scattered helter-skelter.

"Now I will sell nothing today," he complained, feeling very sorry for himself. "Nobody will come to buy things that are broken and soiled. I might as well go out of business."

Felix and Roger began to pick things up. As Mr. Chew pointed with his finger to show them where things belonged, they put things back as well as they could.

Mr. Chew kept on talking to himself. "When my friend, Joe Ming, comes by," he said, "I will ask him to keep shop for me. Then I will go to see Mr. Fong at that restaurant." He sat down on the stool in his little booth, took up a Chinese newspaper, and ignoring the boys, started to read.

Felix turned to Roger. "I don't want to go to Chinese school," he said, "and I don't want to go home."

"Come home with me then," said Roger. "My mother has a dress factory right up this hill. Come and let my mother help you. Maybe you have broken some bones."

Limping, Felix went to the factory with Roger. All the women at their sewing machines stopped their laughing and chattering and stared at him. Roger told his mother what had happened and she took Felix in the kitchen at the back. She made the boy lie down on a cot while she examined him. He had no broken bones but he hurt and ached all over. She told him to lie still and rest while she prepared dinner. Then he sat up and ate with Roger's family. They ate early so Roger could go to Chinese school.

Roger's father said to Felix, "Now you must go home and tell your father."

Felix was grateful to Roger and his family for their kindness. He thanked them and went out into the street. He stared walking, but not in the direction of home. How could he go there? Mei Gwen would already have told Mother what had happened. Mr. Chew of the wall-shop would have visited Father at the Lotus Garden Restaurant and demanded damages. Father could be very severe when one of his sons got into serious trouble.

No, Felix could not go home—at least, not right now. He put his hand in his pocket. Luckily he had money. Roger's route manager had paid the boys off before they started on their route. If he could not go home, where could he go? There was only one place he wanted to go, the place that had filled his thoughts and dreams ever since he left there many months before. He walked down to the end of Commercial Street and kept on walking until he came to the Bay Bridge Terminal at First and Mission Streets. He boarded a bus that said *Alameda* on the front. It was crowded and he had a hard time finding a seat. He did not see the other passengers, nor did he look out of the windows. His mind was filled with the thought of Alameda. He hated San Francisco and never wanted to see it again.

The bus seemed slow to Felix and he thought it would never get there. After crossing the bridge to Oakland, it turned south and began making frequent stops. When it came to the big park in Alameda, Felix got off. He was now about two miles from his former home.

He remembered how he used to take his younger brothers to

the park, and how he brought a compass along, so they would not get lost. He brought chalk and string too, to mark the trees along the streets. He chuckled to himself over his childish idea of "safety first." The houses along the way looked pretty much the same and he knew what direction to go. His legs grew more and more tired, so he found it hard to keep going. But he felt happier now that he knew he would soon be there.

He thought about the plum tree as he walked along. Once when he was halfway up the tree, his foot got stuck in a crotch. He tried to get it loose. He pulled so hard that he pulled his foot out of the shoe, fell to the ground and landed on his back. His shoe was still stuck up in the tree and he had given himself a bad jolt. He thought of Grandma Reed and the magic bird and how he had wounded it.

Felix grew more and more tired the farther he walked. But at last he reached the heart of Alameda. When he passed the public library and the police station with the big Christmas tree in front, he forgot his fatigue and quickened his steps. Now he was almost there. Down at the corner by the *Times* building, he turned into the narrow little side street. The first thing he saw was a flock of pigeons in the sky. They swooped down and landed in the street beyond. Were they Uncle Marvin's?

Felix had decided to go to Cousin Hom's. He would feel at home there in the same house, the same rooms, the same yard, and on the same street where he had lived before. He would visit Cousin Hom and his wife and see all his old friends again—Johnny Lew and Timmy Reed and Jack Bailey and the others. He would be happy again as he had never been since the family had moved to San Francisco.

Felix rubbed his eyes. Was he in the wrong street? What had happened? Where were the houses? Where was Johnny Lew's house and Jack Bailey's? What he saw now was a big open space across from Cousin Hom's. On it he saw a large sign on posts, which read: PARKING LOT—25¢ per hour. The houses were gone. They had been moved away or torn down. The boy's heart skipped a beat.

Even here, in his dream-place, in Alameda, could changes come? Only a short time ago, when he came in Uncle Ed's truck, he had been so sure—Alameda was just the same, it had not changed at all. How could this well-loved neighborhood change like this? Was Alameda turning into a big city, too? Would it never be "country" any more?

But on his own side, on Cousin Hom's side, the houses were still there, Grandpa Reed's, Cousin Hom's and Old Man Tracy's. It was nearly dark now, and there were lights shining in the Reeds' house and the Tracys'. But Cousin Hom's house was dark. Cousin Hom and his wife must be in the kitchen, preparing supper. Felix ran lightly up the steps and knocked at the front door.

But no answer came. He knocked again—*They must be there.* But he heard no sound. *They must be home, they've got to be at home, after I've come all this long way,* thought Felix. He ran down the steps, opened the side gate and ran along the board walk to the back yard, but the yard was empty, too. Weeds and grass grew high. The fishpool had no water and no fish in it—it was only an empty cement shell. *Where were they? Where had they gone?* Felix looked more closely now. Running up the back steps, he peered in at the kitchen window. There was no furniture inside. They had moved away.

He sat on the back step and hid his face in his hands. He sat there for a long time, letting the hard facts sink in. Alameda the beautiful, Alameda his old home was not the same. It would never be the same again. All the things about it that he had known and loved so much, that he had longed for and dreamed about, were changed and gone. Change, change, was life nothing but change? Was growing up nothing but change? As he sat there, Felix changed from a boy to a man. He knew now that he had to give up the thought of Alameda. Cured of his homesickness, he would somehow have to begin life over again. How, he did not know. For now, all that he could feel was the pain and the sorrow of the experience.

He sat there for a long time, and he knew that he was very tired. He looked up and saw that darkness had come. Across the high board fence, he saw a light in the Reeds' kitchen. Inside, he saw Grandma Reed moving about, washing dishes. He thought of all her kindness in the past. Never had she given him a cross word. He knew she would take him in and give him food to eat and a place to sleep. She would ask no questions, but she would think it very strange that he should be here so late at night, strange that he did not know Cousin Hom had moved away. These questions would be in her eyes even if she did not say them, and they would be hard to explain.

Suddenly he was fearful for the Reeds. Would their house be torn down too, and would they have to move away? That would be hard for them after living here for thirty years. Where would they go, now that they were so old?

Wearily, Felix made his way around to the front of the house. Should he go to Uncle Marvin's on Central Avenue, a block away? The new parking lot extended over to the back of Uncle Marvin's yard. The pigeon houses inside the fence were exposed to view. It was only a short walk across to his back door. At least Uncle Marvin still had his laundry and home, still had his pigeons. But how long could he keep them?

What would Uncle Marvin say if Felix came to his door and knocked? How could Felix explain what he was doing here in Alameda, alone, at night? Uncle Marvin was Father's elder brother, more severe even than Father. How could he say that he had run away from home and that Father did not know where he was? Uncle Marvin would take him back to San Francisco, to

Father without delay. No—there would be no food, no bed and no rest at Uncle Marvin's house tonight.

Felix walked along the narrow little street. Old Man Tracy's house was dark—he had gone to bed. A cold breeze was blowing in from the bay. The boy shivered with the dampness. Beyond Tracys' yard, there were more changes. The old wooden store buildings were torn down and being replaced. A large new cement block garage had been built at the corner. On the street side it was a gas station, brightly lighted, with a number of gasoline pumps and several busy attendants in uniform. Inside a wide door opening on the little side street, mechanics were working. It was warm there, so Felix slipped inside the door. No one noticed him. A noisy machine was throwing off a wave of heat. Felix held out his hands. He stayed there and the heat warmed him through and through.

He tried not to think what would happen next.

CHAPTER X

A Day of Understanding

That afternoon, when Mei Gwen reached the jeans factory, Mother stood waiting at the door.

"We have had an accident," said Mother. "Please be kind to Jessie Chong. Her mother ran a needle into her finger and had to be taken to the Chinese hospital. She may not be able to sew for a while."

Mei Gwen said, "O. K." She disliked Jessie, but had no time to think of her now. All that mattered was Elder Brother. The words "arrested" and "in jail" kept ringing in the girl's ears. It was so dreadful, she could not tell Mother. Hers was a heavy secret to keep.

Mei Gwen hoped Mother would stop work and go home early today. She could hardly wait to get home. Maybe Felix would be there waiting. Maybe he would say it was not true at all. There had been no policeman, no angry shopkeeper, no baskets and souvenirs thrown on the sidewalk. It was all just a bad dream.

She followed her mother into the dark factory interior. Frankie ran ahead saying, "Shall I open the light?" He turned on the shaded light over Mother's sewing machine and she started to work.

Mei Gwen sat down on a bench at the back, near a huge pile of blue denim. All the men and women were sewing busily. The room was noisy with the roaring and vibration of the machines. Frankie and Freddie were playing cowboy with Jessie's brother Jimmy, on the men's side. Freddie leaped on the red hobbyhorse and jumped off. Jimmy came behind. He leaped on, jumped up and down a few times, then chased the other boys in and around the sewing machines. The game ended in a fight, with Jimmy and Freddie on top of Frankie, pounding him hard. Uncle Leon sent them all outside.

The younger children crowded around Mei Gwen. Jessie had been trying to take her place, but they were used to Mei Gwen and her ways.

"Tell us a story," cried Cousin Dorinda. "Tell us about the princess."

"Not today," said Mei Gwen. "I don't feel like it. Some other time."

"Take us around the block," cried the children. "Let's play *Shake, shake, shake.*"

"Not today," said Mei Gwen again.

Then Jessie Chong came in. She did not look sad and she had not been crying. Maybe she did not care if her mother ran a needle through her finger. Of course, thought Mei Gwen, women who did not know how to sew ought to stay away from a jeans factory—and keep their children away, too.

Jessie came boldly up to Mei Gwen.

"What are you doing here?" she asked. "Why aren't you at Chinese school?"

"I'll go when I get ready," said Mei Gwen.

"You're playing hookey, I see," said Jessie. "That's bad to play hookey from Chinese school, because your mother has to pay money for you to go there. Your mother works hard and you just waste her money, don't you?"

Mei Gwen's mother called over to the girls. "Who's going to get our coffee today?"

Jessie and Mei Gwen looked at each other.

Mei Gwen did not jump up quickly. Her face fell and she called back, "Oh, let Jessie go!"

"You don't want to?" asked Jessie. "If you hurry, you can get back in plenty of time for Chinese school."

Mei Gwen got up and turned her back. "Go ahead," she said.

Mother Fong gave Jessie the coffeepot and the money and returned to her sewing machine. Jessie went out, with the little children following.

After they left, Mei Gwen went to the small room at the back of the factory. Susie was taking her nap in the playpen as usual. Aunty Rose, who had been doing accounts at her desk, got up and went over to the women's side. No one spoke to Mei Gwen or noticed her. Down in a dark corner, behind some bundles of jeans, she took out a box from a carton.

It was a beautiful box of inlaid wood. Once long ago, Grandmother Yee had given it to the girl for a birthday gift. It was Mei Gwen's treasure box. She opened it and spread out her treasures. There were gold and silver stars and Christmas trees that Edith had given her; some shiny colored papers from Mr. Pete, a pretty paper doily, a Chinese puzzle and an imitation gold motto bracelet. In the bottom part was her red rubber ball and a handful of jacks. Mei Gwen put the bracelet on her arm and looked at the locket on it, with a heart in the center. Around the locket were the words:

May we love as long as we live,
May we live as long as we love.

Mei Gwen read the motto over and over. Uncle Fred had given

her the bracelet last year for Christmas. She liked to pretend it was real gold. She wore it only on special occasions.

"Mei Gwen! Mei Gwen!" She heard Aunty Rose calling her.

Quickly she put the ball and jacks in her pocket, replaced her treasures and closed the sliding cover of the box. She put it deep down in the carton and covered it up with her old coat. She did not want the little children to find it or Jessie Chong to know she had it.

"Mei Gwen!" called Aunty Rose at the door. "Look at the clock. You are already fifteen minutes late for Chinese school."

"I hate Chinese school," said Mei Gwen. "I'm not going today."

"Well, if you're not going," said Aunty Rose, "you might work a little while. Come and do some stapling—we've got a rush order on."

Mei Gwen walked leisurely over to the stairs. She heard the women asking for their coffee. They said they were tired of waiting. Finally Jessie Chong came in with it and set it down. The little ones crowded round her.

"Give us one! Give us one!" they cried.

Mei Gwen stood still and watched. Jessie took a large paper tablet out from under her arm and an envelope from her pocket. Mei Gwen knew where Jessie had been, even before she began to pass out sheets of paper, and before she took the gold stars out of the envelope. Jessie had stopped to see Edith and had called up under Mr. Pete's window. Edith and Mr. Pete liked Jessie too! Well—what of it? What did it matter, anyway? Felix was in trouble—that was the important thing. Mei Gwen tried to keep her mind on Elder Brother, but she couldn't. She had to have it out with Jessie, once and for all. She stepped forward where Jessie could see her.

"So you've taken my job away from me, Jessie Chong!" she said. "You think you are baby sitter around here now, don't you?"

"When you started going to Chinese school," said Jessie quietly, "there was no one to look after the little children but me."

"Did Aunty Rose tell you to do it?" asked Mei Gwen.

"Yes, she did," said Jessie, "and I told her I'd help her."

"Does she pay you for it?"

"Fifty cents a week," said Jessie.

"O. K. then," said Mei Gwen. "It's your job."

Aunty Rose came up. "What's the matter here? You girls quarreling?"

"No," said Mei Gwen. "I've just been hearing the latest news."

Aunty Rose looked from one girl to the other. Then she said to Mei Gwen, "Jessie's been so good about helping with the little children. She's as good a baby sitter as you."

"Is that *so*?" said Mei Gwen.

Tears came to Jessie's eyes, but she said nothing.

"Yes, it's true," said Aunty Rose.

"Then I've lost my job, have I?" asked Mei Gwen.

"I'm afraid you have," said Aunty Rose. "You can't look after the children while you're in Chinese school, can you?"

"I hate Chinese school," said Mei Gwen.

"I can't help that," said Aunty Rose, walking away.

All at once, Mei Gwen crumpled up. She sat down on a pile of jeans and began to cry, hiding her face in her hands. Cousin Dorinda came up and said, "Don't cry, Mei Gwen." The other little ones crowded around her, showing their gold stars. At least they still loved her. The little children went away and she was left alone. She listened to the roar and vibration of the machines. Then she felt an arm around her neck. Looking up, she saw that it was Jessie. She turned away, but Jessie held her tight.

"I didn't want to take your job away from you," said Jessie. "I knew how much you like the little kids."

Mei Gwen sobbed and did not look up.

"I never asked Edith and Mr. Pete to give me things," Jessie went on. "Honest, I didn't, Mei Gwen. I never asked Aunty Rose for this job either."

"I know you didn't, Jessie," said Mei Gwen when she could talk. Suddenly all the old bitterness was gone. "I was only kidding you." She cried a while, then she added, "I'm sorry your mother hurt her finger, Jessie." Jessie gave her a hug.

"Tell us a story, Mei Gwen," begged Cousin Dorinda and the little ones, coming back in.

"Jessie will tell you a story," said Mei Gwen, getting up. "I have to do some stapling for Aunty Rose."

Back at the apartment late that afternoon, Mother was cross because Mei Gwen had stayed away from Chinese school. It seemed very quiet there with only Mother and little Susie and the two younger boys. Every time she heard a sound, Mei Gwen thought it was Felix coming in. She kept watching the clock. She knew he could not get home until after Chinese school—nearly eight. It seemed a long time to wait. She sent Frankie and Freddie down to the front door to watch for him. Ellen and Elaine, the twins from across the hall, came over to play, but Mei

Gwen sent them home. She had not the heart to make up games. She sat on the kitchen floor and played jacks, while Mother started the evening meal.

The garbage can was full, so Mother told Mei Gwen to take it down to the back yard. Mei Gwen hated to go down the open zigzag back stairs. There were thirty-six of them and they were so narrow, winding and steep they made her dizzy. Up on the top floor, she felt safely remote from the neighbors. But on the back stairs, passing the open doors to their kitchens, she could hear what they were saying and doing. She felt as if she were intruding into their private lives. She picked up the heavy can and started down.

In the Yang apartment on the third floor, Lester had his telescope and was looking out the back window, across the bay. His supper was on the table and his mother was scolding him for not coming to eat. Across the hall, Mrs. Ping was having trouble with her electric washer. It was flooding the floor and soapy water ran down the back steps and made them slippery. On the second floor, the radio was playing very loud, so people would not hear Mr. and Mrs. Quan quarreling again. The Sungs' kitchen smelled of fish which Sandra was frying. She put her head out and asked Mei Gwen to stay for supper, but she shook her head and went on.

Mei Gwen walked past old Mr. Wong's back door and the landlord's. She could hear Mr. Wong playing Chinese music, but she did not stop. Four more steps took her down to the back yard, where the large garbage cans were. She opened one and dumped her garbage in. Several cats came up and rubbed against her legs. She wondered who they belonged to. Mei Gwen picked

one of them up—a little gray kitten. She looked at the others, the old ones.

"You mustn't make so much noise at night," she said. "It keeps us awake and it makes my father angry. He will pour water down on your backs if you do it any more."

She petted the fuzzy little kitten. It was much nicer than a pet chicken. The kitten curled up in her arms and began to purr. On her way back, Mr. Wong opened his door and called to her. He wore a black skullcap and a long black Chinese gown. He had a wispy white beard.

"You want to play my harp?" he asked.

"I can't stay long, Mr. Wong," said Mei Gwen.

She set her garbage can down and put the kitten on Mr. Wong's bed. She sat down on a stool, took the tiny bamboo sticks in her

hands and tapped lightly on the strings. The wooden body of the instrument was shaped like a butterfly.

Mr. Wong laughed and said, "You do it better every time. Soon you will make real Chinese music. Now I have something for you. Please take it to your mother with my compliments."

He brought a ripe winter melon and laid it in her hands.

"But how can I carry the kitten and the garbage can and the melon?" asked Mei Gwen, laughing.

"I will put the melon in a paper sack for you," said Mr. Wong.

"Thank you very much," said the girl.

Mei Gwen counted the steps as she went back up, hoping not to drop anything. Mother was pleased to have the gift of the melon. Mei Gwen sat on the davenport and played with the kitten. She tied a pink ribbon around its neck. But she did not forget Felix. Eight o'clock came and went. Then Father came home. They ate and Mei Gwen started to dry dishes.

"Where is my eldest son?" asked Father suddenly.

Mei Gwen, nervous and tense, dropped a rice bowl. It fell to the floor with a clatter and broke into pieces. Mother scolded her for being careless and the tears began to come. Mei Gwen ran to the front room, picked up the kitten from the davenport and began to pet it.

"Whose cat is that?" asked Father sternly.

"I don't know . . ." said Mei Gwen. "Maybe the landlord . . ."

"Where did you find it?" demanded Father.

"Down in the back yard when I emptied the garbage," said Mei Gwen.

"Take it down and put it where you found it," said Father.

"Do not bring stray alley cats into our home."

Mei Gwen cried all the way down the thirty-six steps and all the way up again. She hated to part with the kitten, but she told herself she was crying, not for the kitten, but for Elder Brother. Her important secret grew heavier by the minute. How could she tell Father that Felix would not come home tonight because the policeman had arrested him and put him in jail? No—no—a little girl could not tell her father that. Instead, she went quietly to the bathroom, undressed for bed, crawled into her cot and cried herself to sleep. Once toward morning she thought she heard a bell ringing and someone talking a long time on the telephone. But she was too sleepy to listen.

The next morning Mei Gwen looked in to see Felix's bed. It was empty—Felix had not come home all night. The girl looked at Mother, but Mother said nothing. Was Mother's face pale and were her lips a little tight? Why had Father left earlier than usual? Why wouldn't Mother talk? Did Father and Mother know that Felix was in jail? Had Father gone to get him out?

Mei Gwen's eyes filled with tears. She could not eat her breakfast and Mother scolded her. Mother packed the children's school lunches and put clean shirts on Frankie and Freddie. Then she wasted no time in sending the three children off to school.

That afternoon, Mei Gwen went straight from school to the jeans factory, but Mother was not there.

Uncle Leon met her at the door and asked, "Has Felix come home yet?"

"I don't know," said Mei Gwen.

"Is your father home yet?" he asked.

"I don't know," said Mei Gwen.

"When a family has trouble," said Aunty Rose, bustling up, "we must all stand together. I will send the workers home and go to my sister. I must give her advice and comfort."

"Now that is foolish, Rose," said Uncle Leon. "The worst is over by now. You always exaggerate everything. Besides, the workers do not like to be laid off for even part of a day. And it will make me late in filling our orders."

"At other jeans factories around here," said Aunty Rose, "they work long hours, on day and night shifts. But we are easy on them, we give them piece work—they work only as much as they please. They are always taking time off to stay home for any old excuse. Today, I will send them home early, when we are in trouble."

Mei Gwen looked from her aunt to her uncle. She did not understand what they were arguing about.

"Run along home quickly, Mei Gwen," said Aunty Rose. "Your mother needs you. Stop at Aunty Kate's and take Grandmother Yee with you. At a time like this, we all need Grandmother's advice and wisdom to guide us."

"Is he . . . Is Elder Brother . . . in jail?" asked Mei Gwen, bursting into tears. "Can't Father get him out?" But Aunty Rose and Uncle Leon had rushed off to talk to the workers and did not answer her.

Jessie Chong came running up. Seeing Mei Gwen in tears, she put her arm around her. "You are my best girl-friend," she said. "Do not cry—I love you. . . ."

Jessie walked with Mei Gwen as far as Aunty Kate's Beauty Parlor. Mei Gwen went in, but Aunty Kate and Grandmother

Yee were not there. The young lady in charge said they had left an hour before.

When Mei Gwen reached home, a family conference was going on. Aunty Kate and Mother and Grandmother Yee and Uncle Fred were all standing in the front room talking. They were soon joined by Aunty Rose and Uncle Leon. When Mei Gwen came in, they sent her out. She went back to the kitchen and sat on the floor. She played jacks a while and tried not to think of Felix. When Ellen and Elaine, the twins, came in, she played *Shake, shake, shake* with them. Frankie and Freddie were sent into the kitchen, too, and told to stay there. They all played school and Mei Gwen was the teacher. She scolded and spanked her pupils so hard that they all began screaming. Mother came and told them to be quiet.

Late in the afternoon, Father and Uncle Marvin and Felix came home. They went into the front room and the door was closed behind them.

Not until long afterward did Mei Gwen know what had happened.

While Felix was warming his hands in the mechanic's garage the night before, he noticed a truck parked in the corner of the building. Suddenly someone in front turned the lights out. He made his way to the truck in the darkness, opened the door of the cab and climbed in. He curled up on the seat and fell asleep.

About five in the morning, the garage came to life again. Lights were turned on, a mechanic came in and walked to the truck. Felix was awakened when a light was flashed into his face.

"A Chinese kid!" said the man. "Asleep in my truck! How did you get in here, kid? I locked the outside door myself last night."

"I came in before you locked the door," said Felix.

"Come on now, get down," said the man. "I've got to work on that truck."

Felix climbed down, looked out the window and saw it was still dark. He did not know what to do or where to go. He began to feel hungry. The mechanic backed the truck around, opened the hood and set to work, whistling. Felix sat down on an oil barrel and watched him.

"Say, kid, I bet you're hungry, ain't you?" asked the man.

Felix nodded. The man went to his lunch box, took out a hot dog and handed it to the boy. Felix gobbled it down.

"Thanks," he said.

"Don't you think you'd better be goin' wherever you're goin'?" asked the mechanic. "Won't your folks be expectin' you?"

"No," said Felix. "I'm not going anywhere."

"You any relation to that Chinese laundryman around the corner on Central Avenue?" asked the man.

Felix looked at the floor and said nothing. He knew the man meant Uncle Marvin.

"Where do you live?" asked the man.

Again Felix did not answer. He decided that he would leave the garage as soon as daylight came. He would go somewhere—anywhere.

Whistling cheerfully, the man went into the gas station in front. It had opened up, and the attendants were coming in. Felix could hear them laughing and joking with each other. He sat still, leaning against the wall, trying to figure out what to do. He dozed again, still tired and sleepy.

Suddenly he heard a familiar voice. He jumped to his feet and there stood Uncle Marvin Fong—just the person he did not want to see. The mechanic must have telephoned him.

"Hello, Felix," said Uncle Marvin. "What are you doing here?"

Felix hung his head and did not reply.

"He's my nephew, Felix Fong," Uncle Marvin told the mechanic. "My brother and his family used to live back on this little street, and the boy always liked it here. Our Cousin Hom has just moved out of the Fong house. Felix came over to visit him, didn't you, Felix?" He made it sound quite natural that a boy should be away from his home all night.

Felix did not answer. He saw Uncle Marvin go to the telephone and put through a call to Father Fong, but he could not hear what he said. He heard Uncle Marvin thank the mechanic for notifying him. Then he followed Uncle Marvin home.

Uncle Marvin's wife was kind and set out food. But Felix could not eat and, somehow, he could not talk. When Aunty Lucy offered to show him the pigeons, Felix would not even look at them. He sat down on a couch and soon fell over in a deep sleep. He slept until the middle of the afternoon. When he awoke, he heard Uncle Marvin telephoning Father again. Aunty Lucy brought him food and he ate.

By this time, Felix knew that he had to go home again. He did not much care what happened to him. He could not seem to think for himself. It was easier to do what he was told to do. So before he realized it, he was riding the bus back to San Francisco, with Uncle Marvin at his side. They stopped first at the Lotus Garden Restaurant and picked up Father.

When they reached the apartment, Felix walked wearily up the stairs. A family conference was going on in the front room, with Grandmother Yee and the aunts and uncles there. The boy sat down on a chair near the fireplace and listened. Across the room, over the davenport, hung the life-sized portraits of his Fong grandparents. As the others talked, the boy could hear Grandfather Fong and all his grandfathers before him talking. He knew that he was one link in the long chain of the Fong family ancestry. He felt the heavy burden of his inheritance on his shoulders. Grandfather Fong kept on looking at him and talking to him in plain words.

Felix listened to all that was said, and answered questions as well as he could. He felt free to talk now. He wanted to get the whole thing over with. He wanted to begin all over again—with the regained love and respect of his family. They did not make him feel a culprit. They tried to rebuild his own self-respect.

The boy was surprised to learn several things—that Father had stayed out all night hunting for him and that Roger and Roger's parents had told Father about the scooter mishap. Mr. Chew had come to see Father and reported the damage done to the wall-shop, but wanted no trouble made over it. The aunts and uncles had all decided that Mr. Chew should be paid for all the ruined stock. They also decided to give the wall-shop as much business as possible and to send their friends there to buy. This would help to restore his prestige in the neighborhood.

No one asked Felix why he went to Alameda. They all seemed to know and to think it unfortunate that Cousin Hom had been so remiss as to move away to Berkeley without telling the family. Aunty Kate could not understand why Felix had not gone to Uncle Marvin's and telephoned at once, instead of upsetting the whole family. Uncle Leon made light of the whole misadventure and made them all laugh when he said, "If it had been me, I'd never have stopped until I got to New York!"

At last the conference was over and they all went home—all but Grandmother Yee.

Mei Gwen met Felix in the hall. He was surprised to see that she had been crying. "What's the matter, Younger Sister?" he asked.

"Oh, you were gone so long . . ." she said.

Felix was greatly moved to see that she cared so much. "They did not tell you?"

"Did you stay in jail all night?" she asked, her eyes wide with fear.

"No, Younger Sister," said Felix tenderly. "I spent the night in Alameda, but I don't think I'll ever do it again."

"Are you going to stay home with us now?" asked Mei Gwen.

"Yes, Younger Sister," said Felix.

"I'm glad," said Mei Gwen.

After the others were gone, Felix sat on the davenport beside Grandmother Yee. She held his hands in hers, and he listened as she talked.

"When I first came to San Francisco, I hated it here, too," she said. "In China I had always lived in the country and never in the city. I did not like the noise and the rush and the terrible crowding—many families lived in a single room then. I got a job in a factory and had to learn to sew on a sewing machine. I had never seen machines before and I was afraid of them. They went so fast by electricity and roared so loud. I cried every day to go back to China, back to the country where one could see and live with growing things—where a girl could pick a flower and put it in her hair . . .

"My son, you have been homesick for Alameda. To be a Chinese is to be homesick. Every Chinese has a deep longing within him to return to the place of his birth. All his life he dreams of his native village, no matter how humble—of the hut with mud walls and dirt floor, of the flowering plum tree, the red tile roof of the courtyard and the singing birds. Our children and grandchildren, though born in a foreign country, still look upon China as our homeland and will cleave to it until death. But now that our country is in the hands of the enemy and we can no longer go home to die on native soil, there is but one thing to do—make this new land our own."

"The Alameda I loved is gone, Grandmother," said Felix. "I don't want to see it again."

"Here, then, is your homeland," said Grandmother, "here in the big city of San Francisco. There are things to love here if we look for them." Pointing to a fuchsia plant blooming on the window sill, she added, "A flower is better to look at than a stone wall."

Felix smiled, trying to understand.

"But Father, is he not angry?" asked Felix. "Is he not going to punish me?"

"Your father is a man of wisdom," said Grandmother. "He knows when you have punished yourself enough. He knows when you have taught yourself a lesson."

"And Mr. Chew—" asked Felix. "Will he forgive me, too?"

"The next time you deliver his newspaper," said Grandmother, "Mr. Chew will smile and offer you a handful of lichee nuts. In this life there is only one thing to do, repay evil with good."

CHAPTER XI

A Day of New Beginnings

"O Mother, the flowers smell so sweet!"

Mei Gwen set the bowl of blooming narcissus on the window sill. She sniffed their sweet fragrance.

"Bring the dustpan and the dustcloth," called Mother. "The house must be cleaned before midnight. Then we will hide the brooms away."

Mother was cleaning the front room and Mei Gwen hurried to help. The floor had been washed and polished. All the furniture had been moved and needed dusting. The other rooms were spick-and-span. There was new oilcloth on the kitchen table and there were new curtains at the windows. Mother had stayed home from the factory and worked hard all week.

It was February and Chinese New Year was at hand. Everything had to be neat and clean before New Year's Eve. That was the way to bring good luck for the coming year.

"New Year is the day of the Three Beginnings," said Grandmother Yee, "the start of the year, of the month, and of the season. It is the time when we all make a new start in life."

Mei Gwen could not keep her mind on dusting. She was longing to see her new Chinese costume.

"When is Aunty Kate coming?" she asked. "And will she bring it?"

Grandmother smiled. "She will soon be here."

When Aunty Kate came they all gathered round to see Mei Gwen's costume and said, "How beautiful!" The costume had long trousers to the ankles and a short-sleeved jumper that fastened at the neck and down one side. It was made of yellow satin and was embroidered with flowers and a large bird.

"Is it Felix' magic bird?" asked Mei Gwen.

"The queen bird, or phoenix," said Grandmother Yee, "has five colors—green, yellow, black, red and white. The bird in the plum tree stands for the springtime of life. It means youth and hope and everything new. The good earth blooms again with the return of the birds."

Mei Gwen tried on her new costume. She walked in and out of the rooms while the family admired it.

"All debts must be paid before New Year's," said Father. "Then one can go through the new year an honorable man."

Father took Felix with him to the shops where he owed money. Red silk banners hung in doorways, with mottoes in Chinese characters painted upon them. Felix read them to Father: *"Peaceableness brings good luck. One who is contented is always happy. Patience is the best family heritage."* The Chinese merchants greeted Father Fong ceremoniously. They shook hands with Felix, his eldest son, and after accepting payment, offered cups of hot tea.

Felix had never seen Grant Avenue look so festive. Chinatown itself was transformed. All the shops had been cleaned, and new and unusual delicacies were displayed. Hampers of fresh green and white vegetables and baskets of unique dried seafoods lined the already crowded sidewalks. Huge branches of blossoming cherry, almond and plum trees had been placed on sale. Pots of blooming azaleas, camellias, gardenias and other plants were standing on benches. Fresh oranges and tangerines were piled high in show windows. Brightly lighted Chinese lanterns swayed back and forth under awnings and inside doorways.

The shops were crowded with eager purchasers and there was much noise and excitement. Firecrackers were popping on all sides, making people laugh and jump nervously. Everyone was in a festive mood. Felix saw Roger Loy go by with his father, and Ronnie Chow with his. The boys smiled at each other and said formally, "Happy New Year."

Father Fong and Felix stopped at the Lee Hop Wall-shop. Mr. Chew, too, had blooming plants on his shelves. After an exchange of greetings, Father looked them over carefully.

"A plum tree is the symbol of spring," said Mr. Chew.

Father agreed. He purchased a huge branch covered with buds, and two pots of red azaleas. They carried them home and decorated the front room with them. Earlier in the week, Father had bought the groceries necessary for the New Year's meals, and a plentiful supply of fresh oranges and tangerines. These he piled in neat pyramids on platters on the tables. One table in the front room was covered with a red embroidered silk tablecloth which Mother had brought from China. This table held small dishes of sweetmeats of all kinds. Red silk hangings and pillow covers gave the room a festive air. Red silk scarves were draped over the portraits of the Fong grandparents above the davenport.

At last, when all the preparations were completed, Father placed a tangerine with a leaf and branch attached, on the head of the Buddha on the mantelpiece. Outdoors the shooting of firecrackers, to drive away evil spirits, became louder. The banging and popping continued far into the night, so there was little sleep for anyone. At midnight, the shops on Grant Avenue were closed, and the streets were cleared of stalls and hucksters, in preparation for the approaching holiday.

New Year's Day dawned clear and bright. It was given over to visiting. The Fong family had many callers. Mei Gwen wore her Chinese costume and passed the sweetmeats—candied cocoanut, strips of winter melon, candied and pickled plums, cumquats, lichee nuts and melon seeds. Mother poured tea for her guests, passed oranges and tangerines and special cakes. She gave all the children who came money wrapped in red Chinese paper.

Aunty Rose and Uncle Leon came with the cousins, Dorinda, Paul and Jean. The children played in the hall while the grown people visited. Little Susie's face was dirty, so Mei Gwen took her to the bathroom and washed it. Dorinda picked up the wet washcloth and began to play ball with it. Running into the front room, she threw it to Susie. Susie was too little to catch it and it fell on the red silk tablecloth. Aunty Rose rushed over, scolded the children, and tried to dry the spot on the cloth.

Mother Fong said sadly, "It is my best cloth. I brought it from China and now it is spoiled."

Other friends and relatives came—the Sungs from downstairs, the Yicks from across the hall, and a number of the women who worked at the factory with their husbands and children. Among them were the Chongs with Jessie and Jimmy and younger children. To all, Mother was courteous and polite, offering tea, and Father talked and exchanged greetings. To all, Mei Gwen passed sweetmeats and fruit.

Late on the second day came the parade. Mei Gwen and Felix left the apartment early and went to the meeting place at their Chinese school. The parade started on Stockton Street and went through the tunnel, then down Sutter Street and up Grant Avenue. There were two floats, several bands and drum corps and two Chinese Lions, followed by groups of Chinese children and various organizations.

Thousands of people, American and Chinese, lined the streets. Some were on stairs, some on balconies or boxes. Some climbed poles, while others were looking from windows, fire escapes and roofs. Many people took pictures and movies. They all stretched their necks to get a good view of the parade.

Mei Gwen was a princess and she looked and acted like one. Dressed in her beautiful costume, she carried a lighted Chinese lantern and wore flowers in her hair. All the girls in her class carried lanterns and wore flowers. They looked so pretty, the crowd on the sidewalk clapped as they passed by.

Sandra Sung walked beside Mei Gwen. Since her mother's recovery, she, too, had started to Chinese school. Her costume was a soft green, trimmed with shining sequins.

"Oh, I'm cold!" said Sandra. The sun had set and a chilly breeze was blowing. "I wish I'd brought my sweater."

"I'm not cold," said Mei Gwen. "I'm too excited to be cold." Just then she sneezed loudly. "If we wore our sweaters or coats, the people couldn't see our pretty Chinese costumes."

The wind blew a strong gust and the candle in Mei Gwen's lantern flickered out. "Oh, dear!" she said.

"Hello, Mei Gwen!" A man's voice called from the sidewalk. "You sure do look pretty!"

Mei Gwen looked up at the sea of faces. Suddenly she saw Mr. Pete and Mr. John from the Henderson Paper Company.

They still remembered her. She waved her hand and smiled. Then, not far away, she saw her friend Edith from the Label Company, and the waitress, Tootsie, from Harry's Café. She waved to them all and felt very proud.

"I've got so many American friends," she said to Sandra Sung.

"Where did you get them?" asked Sandra.

"Oh, they work down on the street where my Aunty's jeans factory is," said Mei Gwen.

"I don't know any at all," said Sandra.

The band up ahead burst into a loud din of noisy music, so loud that the girls could not talk. The crowds on the sidewalks grew thicker. The people pushed and shoved and kept moving into the street. Boys on balconies threw firecrackers over people's heads. The little Chinese girls tried to march bravely on, but were halted frequently. They had to stand still, marking time, and all of them were shivering.

"These children will all have pneumonia tomorrow," shouted a Chinese man. Mei Gwen looked—it was Mr. Chew of the wall-shop that Felix had bumped into.

Mei Gwen wondered how Felix was getting along. She looked back but could not see him. He was marching with the School Traffic Squad far behind her. He and the other boys wore white traffic bands and belts, and Felix had been put in charge.

The band music struck up and the parade moved on. Down at the corner near Jackson Street, Mei Gwen saw her own family on the balcony of the Lotus Garden Restaurant. Younger Sister Susie was sitting on Mother's lap, and Father stood by Frankie and Freddie. Aunty Rose and her children were there, and Aunty

Kate, Grandmother Yee and the uncles. Frankie and Freddie were lighting firecrackers and tossing them down. Some caught on a light pole and kept going *pop-pop-pop.*

Mei Gwen waved her hand and called out, "Don't hit me!" She turned to Sandra and said, "See my family up there."

Father shouted, "Are you warm enough?" but the parade was moving on again. They were going north on Grant Avenue toward Little Italy. Suddenly Mei Gwen saw the words *Italian Market* across the top of a store, and there in front on the sidewalk stood Dina Costelli and her family.

"I see my Italian friends," cried Mei Gwen. "They go fishing at Fisherman's Wharf. They are Elder Brother's friends too."

She saw Dina's two brothers, Georgie and Joey, and Dina's father and mother and even her grandmother. Dina pointed out Mei Gwen and they all smiled and waved like old friends.

"Where's Felix?" called Georgie, edging forward on the curb.

Mei Gwen pointed down the street behind her.

"He's marching with the Traffic Squad," she answered.

Georgie nodded and he and Joey started back down the street.

Behind the little Chinese girls came the beautifully lighted Chinese Dragon. The Dragon wore a huge artificial head of many colors, in which bright glass eyes were set above hinged jaws. Behind the head hung a long cloth body of gaily striped satin of many colors, carried aloft by twenty or twenty-five boys. It was an impressive and beautiful sight.

As the Dragon passed, the crowd became very excited. Men and boys threw firecrackers high up in the air or tossed packs of firecrackers from balconies and roofs. Mei Gwen and Sandra became more and more afraid. They clung to each other and wished the people would stop shooting. The crowd grew more dense and the people pressed in closer and closer on the narrow street. The little girls were so squeezed together, there was hardly room for them to march.

"Oh, they're spoiling the parade," cried Sandra in tears.

"Get back, you!" cried Mei Gwen in anger. "Stay on the sidewalk where you belong." But no one heard her.

Suddenly a large firecracker came zooming through the air down toward the street. Mei Gwen's heart skipped a beat, as she jumped back in fright. It exploded in front of her with a loud bang. Mei Gwen dropped her Chinese lantern, for she felt a sharp sting on her hand, where the powder had burned it. She screamed and started to run, but a man had crowded in ahead of her.

The girl looked up and saw her own father. She fell into his arms, shaking with cold and fright, and burst into tears. "Take me home! Take me home!" she cried.

As more firecrackers fell, Father Fong shouted to a noisy group of boys on a near-by balcony, but they paid little attention. Father took Mei Gwen and Sandra out of the parade and told their classmates to go home. He led the two girls through the crowd, saying, "We'll go into the restaurant and wait until the parade is over."

Wading through red firecracker paper deep on the sidewalk, they made their way into the Lotus Garden. There they joined the rest of the family. Father brought salve and bandages from a drugstore, and Mother bound up Mei Gwen's burned hand and arm. It was warm indoors and Sandra and Mei Gwen soon stopped shivering. They all went into a private dining room and had a delicious meal of a variety of dishes—chicken, duck, fresh fish, dried fish soup, bird's-nest soup, diced prawns, Chinese sausages and other good things.

It was late that night when they reached home.

"I heard a little noise," said Mother. "I wonder if there is a mouse in the kitchen."

Felix and Mei Gwen and Mother went out to see.

"Oh, a bird!" cried Mei Gwen. She ran and called Father. "Father, a strange bird flew in our house."

"It is a canary," said Mother. "I left the window open and it flew in from outside."

"Maybe it smelled the lilies on the window sill," said Felix.

The bird flew around the room, then into the hall to the front room. It perched on the branch of the flowering plum tree. When Felix saw it, he stopped and held his breath. He whispered to Younger Sister, "It is like the magic bird in the plum tree at Alameda, but the one I saw before had long feathers in bright colors like the phoenix on your costume."

"A bird is a good omen," said Father. "It will bring us good luck for the New Year. A Chinese home is not complete without a bird in a cage."

"We always had one at home in China," said Mother softly.

Father sent Felix down to the Yangs' apartment, to see if their light was still on, and to try to borrow their bird-cage which they did not use any more. Soon Felix came back with it. When Father caught the bird in his hand, it was shaking with fright. Gently he put it in the cage. Felix gave it crumbs to eat and water to drink. Soon it began to chirp and sing.

"It is happy here," said Felix. "It has forgotten its old home."

Father hung the cage in the bay window, and they all got ready for bed. Mei Gwen's cot was near the fireplace, but that night she could not sleep. She did not like the bird's noise. It kept on chirping and trying to sing, even though she said, "Be quiet." She thought of the chicken on the ranch that kept saying *gyp-gyp-gyp.* She began to cry with fright, calling Mother. When Mother heard what was the matter, she got up and put a dark cloth over the bird's cage.

"Now you can both sleep," she said.

The seven days of the Chinese New Year were busy ones and passed all too quickly. There were Lion Dances daily on the streets, for the Lions were collecting the needed yearly funds for the Chinese hospital. Friends called daily at the Fongs', and they went out returning calls. Wherever they went, the children were given good luck pieces, quarters or half dollars wrapped in red Chinese paper.

One day the Costelli children came to visit the Fong children. Mother cooked Chinese noodles and Won Ton Pay for them, and they said the noodles were as good as Italian spaghetti. The boys got into a friendly quarrel about it. Felix insisted that the Chinese had invented spaghetti, and Georgie insisted it was Italian, so they called Father Fong to settle the matter. He told the boys that when Marco Polo went to China he found it there and brought it back to Italy. So Georgie and Felix were both happy.

Suddenly Mei Gwen exclaimed, "I hear Chinese Lion music!" She put her arm around Dina. "Goody! Goody! The Lion is coming down our street, just so you can see him."

"We must hurry," said Father. "Get the firecrackers."

Felix found a long string, and to the end Father attached lettuce leaves and a tangerine. Coins wrapped in Chinese-red paper were tied under the lettuce leaves, hidden from view. Mei Gwen opened the large window in the bay of the front room, and the boys let the string drop down. It reached to the top of old Mr. Wong's windows on the first floor. The Lion, followed by a noisy crowd and the Lion truck with music, came closer and closer. Felix and Frankie brought out their unused firecrackers, lighted and threw them down. This was to attract the Lion's attention and also to frighten evil spirits away.

The Lion was held up by two young Chinese acrobats. One man held up the head, worked its jaws and reached his hand out through the mouth to take contributions of money. He and his companion, who held up the Lion's tail, danced along the street to the beat of drums, imitating the actions of a real lion.

What fun it was to look down and watch the Lion's antics. He sniffed the air from door to door, shaking his great mane, pretending to took for lettuce leaves. Seeing the decorated string hanging from the Fongs' bay window, he halted, then rushed toward it as the boys' firecrackers burst around his head. Smoke poured out of his nostrils, the Lion music burst forth again, as the great beast swayed and plunged back and forth, circling around the tempting lettuce bait. Suddenly he drew near, leaped upward and snapped his jaws shut over the lettuce leaf and tangerine. The string snapped, he pranced his thanks, then danced onward to the next inviting doorway.

Frankie and Freddie tumbled back on the floor, roaring with

laughter. Georgie pulled the string up and rolled it into a ball.

Joey Costelli cried out, "I'm going to be a Chinese acrobat when I grow up!" This started all the boys doing acrobatic stunts in true Chinese style.

Dina said, "Why don't the Italians have an Italian Lion to dance like that?"

Mei Gwen heard someone crying. Looking around, she found that little Susie had hidden under the bed, frightened. She pulled her out, and Susie helped her pass tangerines and sweetmeats to their guests.

"Felix, when are you going to show us Chinatown?" asked Georgie and Joey.

"Any time you like," said Felix. "What do you want to see?"

"Well—what is there to see?" asked Georgie. "What do you like best yourself?"

The question was a challenge. Felix had to stop and think. Had the time come when he could say that he really liked Chinatown, that he was at home there and loved the big city of San Francisco? What should he tell them?

About the fun of collecting rocks on Russian Hill? About the rollicking rides on the cable cars? About climbing Telegraph Hill for a picnic and seeing the breath-taking view from there? About the playground on Sacramento Street where he had at last made friends with the boys? About the steep Clay Street hill where he met disaster on a borrowed scooter?

Or should he tell them about the kindly shopkeepers and office people and friends along the crowded streets that Roger and Mei Gwen had helped him to know and understand? About that little island of green, Portsmouth Square, where a boy could fly a Chinese kite higher than the trees? Or about the joys of fishing at Fisherman's Wharf which they themselves knew better than he? Should he tell them about the warmth and comfort and good food and understanding in a Chinese home, no different, he was sure, from that in any Italian or any other American home.

Felix hardly knew what he liked best, but one thing was certain. His interests and his loves had spread far beyond the limits of Chinatown. Taken together, in all its many aspects, San Francisco had suddenly become, as Grandmother Yee had predicted, "his homeland." He felt happy and contented now, able to meet whatever came, looking forward eagerly to what the future might bring. He had the heritage of age-old customs and traditions behind him, and the exciting ways of a newer world before him. The combination was a good one.

Chinese New Year was what Grandmother had said—a day of New Beginnings. One thing he knew as he had never known before—the old, restless, gnawing homesickness was gone, and the memory of a happy childhood remained.

"Let's go up to the roof and I'll show you!" said Felix, suddenly inspired.

He and Mei Gwen and Georgie and Joey and Dina climbed the little stairs just as the sun was setting. Lester Yang was there and let them look through his telescope. Now Felix knew, and he pointed out to his friends what he liked best of all—the bay with its boats and fish and bridges, its blue waters and white clouds and gray fogs, and across on the other side, the beloved Alameda of his lost childhood, still alive in his memory.